"Calla…"

Her name on his lips made her decision. She wanted him. She slid into his arms, enjoying the feel of his warm skin against hers. Before he could say anything else, Calla pressed her lips to his.

Kostas's grip tightened as she opened her mouth. His tongue darted across hers, and she sighed. This felt right. It was a fantasy; she knew that. But a fantasy that felt so perfect.

She deepened the kiss. She had less than fifteen hours with Kostas, and she wanted to make them last.

"You're tired." Kostas broke the kiss, his fingers tracing along her side as if he couldn't keep from touching her.

"I don't care." It was the truth. She didn't want to miss whatever chemistry was driving them. Calla could sleep on the plane tomorrow, but something in her screamed that if she missed this opportunity, if she missed being with him, she'd regret it for the rest of her life.

Calla kissed him again, then pulled back. "But if you need sleep…"

He pursed his lips as he stared at her. "I need you."

Dear Reader,

Sometimes a news story happens and with it comes two perfect characters. I read a story about a mother delivering a preterm baby on a plane with NICU professionals headed on vacation. The mother and baby are doing great, and it was described as a miracle that the right combination of professionals was there. With that, the idea for *The Prince's One-Night Baby* was born.

Calla Lewis needs a fresh start following a hard breakup, and a year overseas is the perfect prescription. But leaving home isn't easy. Luckily, she connects with her seatmate, Kostas. Their lives are on separate paths, but for one night, she can lose herself in his arms.

Dr. Kostas Drakos isn't ready to return home. Doctor is the title he's earned, but on Palaío, he's the rebel prince. He's resigned himself to a life of loneliness—until Calla lands at his clinic. Particularly when their one night of passion will bind them together forever.

Calla and Kostas had an instant connection, but it's when they truly get to know each other that love fully grows. I loved giving these two their happily-ever-after. Hope you enjoy *The Prince's One-Night Baby*.

Juliette

THE PRINCE'S
ONE-NIGHT BABY

———

JULIETTE HYLAND

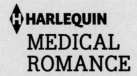

HARLEQUIN

MEDICAL
ROMANCE

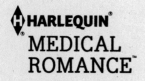

HARLEQUIN®
MEDICAL ROMANCE™

Recycling programs
for this product may
not exist in your area.

ISBN-13: 978-1-335-73748-9

The Prince's One-Night Baby

Harlequin Enterprises ULC
22 Adelaide St. West, 41st Floor
Toronto, Ontario M5H 4E3, Canada
www.Harlequin.com

Printed in U.S.A.

Juliette Hyland began crafting heroes and heroines in high school. She lives in Ohio with her Prince Charming, who has patiently listened to many rants regarding characters failing to follow the outline. When not working on fun and flirty happily-ever-afters, Juliette can be found spending time with her beautiful daughters, giant dogs or sewing uneven stitches with her sewing machine.

Books by Juliette Hyland

Harlequin Medical Romance

Neonatal Nurses

A Nurse to Claim His Heart

Unlocking the Ex-Army Doc's Heart
Falling Again for the Single Dad
A Stolen Kiss with the Midwife
The Pediatrician's Twin Bombshell
Reawakened at the South Pole
The Vet's Unexpected Houseguest

Visit the Author Profile page at Harlequin.com.

For my sister…because she said I had to!

CHAPTER ONE

DR. KOSTAS DRAKOS slid into his first-class seat and immediately put on his headphones. The first leg of his journey from Washington State to his home island of Palaío was almost six hours, and he had no desire to spend any of it talking to a stranger. He had almost twenty-four hours' worth of flights before he got home. Twenty-four hours before Dr. Kostas Drakos reverted from obstetrician to prince. A day before the man he'd become over the last twelve years was thrust back into the royal spotlight full-time.

He pulled up his phone and reread the email from his brother. Ioannis had asked him to return following the retirement of the capital's primary obstetrician. Another might have been able to refuse, but Ioannis wasn't really asking. It was a brother's question couched to hide the summons from the king.

When Ioannis had taken the throne last year, Kostas had returned to the island only long enough to fulfill his sanctioned duties. His brother's son already three, Kostas was currently second in line to the throne. Ioannis's delightful wife, Queen Eleni, was pregnant, and he suspected he'd fall several more spots given the love between Eleni and Ioannis on display for the entire country to see whenever they were ever together.

And that was fine with Kostas.

However, his distance from the crown did not mean he didn't have obligations, as Ioannis's request had gently reminded him. Rolling his shoulders, Kostas tried to get comfortable, though he doubted it was possible, no matter how nice the first-class area was. He was returning to Palaío…returning to the palace…and to the press.

That he'd never sit on the throne hadn't stopped the island's press outlets from speculating about his princess prospects. They'd run headlines for his entire trip about the Prodigal Prince and whether he was finally home to choose a bride. Only his brother's coronation had briefly kicked his name from the front page.

His brother was Palaío's golden child, put on an elevated pedestal at birth. Kostas…well, Kostas was less respected.

Eleni had offered to introduce him to one of her friends so he wouldn't have to attend the coronation alone. She'd told Kostas that the woman was kind and understood that he wasn't staying. No need to worry about a long-term connection.

It had been thoughtful, but there were no short connections with a royal. Royal life had destroyed his mother, and it had burned the one girl he'd gotten attached to as a teenager. Both had left the island following the press's sensational lies.

As the prince, the one born into the family, the press often speculated but kept their cruelest words couched in flowery language. To the best of his knowledge, the one time his teenage love, Maria, had come home, the reporters had met her at the airport. A simple visit to her parents a decade after their connection had resulted in questions about their supposed teenage pregnancy and loss. It was a salacious rumor, made up by a jealous acquaintance, that the media had devoured. He'd been raised to expect his life to belong to the public, but Maria had simply made the mistake of thinking a young prince was cute.

And it had nearly ruined her life.

Kostas had no intention of putting another person in the same position.

When he was on Palaío, he was Prince Kostas. The rebel son, who'd really just wanted to be a regular teen, but they'd thrust microphones in his face and he'd said terse things about his father, about wanting to leave the island, about hating being royal. It had made headlines on the usually quiet island, which meant that his life wasn't truly his. He'd never inherit the throne but he'd always be royal, and that also meant that if he fell in love, the woman would stand beside him in the gilded cage.

He'd serve the clinic for a while, find a new obstetrician, and then head back to Seattle. A year, no more, on the island was all he needed.

A hand touched his shoulder and Kostas jumped, his headphones sliding. He looked up to find a dark-haired beauty staring at him. Her hazel eyes captured his as she held his gaze.

"Can I help you?" The woman was stunning, but she seemed out of place. Her patched-up backpack, her jeans and oversized sweatshirt were not the designer styles he typically saw in first class. *Have I been recognized?*

British royalty fascinated Americans, but they rarely recognized royals from other countries. Still, occasionally someone would know him, and a few women had foolishly hoped the connection might lead to a fantasy ending.

But real royal life wasn't the stuff of television movies. Happily-ever-afters were for other people.

"Um…" She looked at her ticket then up at the seat numbers and back at him, color tinging her cheeks as she bit her lip. "I think you might be in my seat."

"What?" Kostas reached into his back pocket as he saw the flight attendant start toward him.

"I'm 2F, or at least I think I am." She bit her lip, her eyes darting to the flight attendant.

He could see concern floating through her. *Great, a nervous flier.* Hopefully, she'd be all right for their long flight. He didn't really want to deal with the questions and concerns that sometimes came from individuals who rarely took to the skies. It was selfish, he knew it, but Kostas was trying to prep himself for stepping off the plane in Palaío.

"Is there a problem?" The attendant smiled at Kostas as she looked at the woman standing in the aisle, not trying to hide the judgment in her eyes. She saw what Kostas did: a woman out of place.

And they were both assessing her.

Kostas mentally kicked himself. He wasn't in Palaío yet. There was really no reason for his suspicions.

"I…" She looked down at her ticket and then back at the numbers above.

Kostas looked at his ticket and wanted to kick himself even harder. He was in her seat. "No. There isn't a problem. I wasn't paying attention. I'm in 2D not 2F."

He started to stand when the woman held up her hand. "You can stay there. It's okay. Unless you want to move?"

"Can I see your ticket, ma'am?" The flight attendant took a quick look and nodded. "You a standby?"

"Yep," the woman responded, her tone overly bubbly, the kind he heard some of his nurses use when they were trying to put their patients at ease. "Weather canceled my flight, and they told me I could head to New York tomorrow or try to get on tonight as a standby—" She cut her words off and slid into the seat as the attendant wandered off to continue getting ready for takeoff.

Kostas nodded and slid his headphones back on.

"Should have worn something besides the old sweatshirt and comfy jeans, Calla. Maybe then you'd look like you belonged in first class."

The whispered words weren't meant for him. He was sure Calla had assumed he had music or something playing in his headphones. But Kostas had caused the incident that had made her so uncomfortable.

Pulling his headphones off, he turned. First-class seats had more room than business or coach, but he was still uncomfortably close to the woman next to him. She had her eyes closed, and a few tears ran under her glasses and down her cheek, over the freckles dotting her nose.

"I'm sorry." Kostas kept his voice quiet. She was upset, and he knew that when he was upset, the last thing he wanted was an audience. "I am going home. My family's expectations...well, I am a little tense about returning to prying eyes. I took that annoyance out on you. Which is more than a little unfair. There is nothing wrong with how you look."

She wiped her hand across her cheek and offered him a smile. "You're headed home and I'm leaving mine." She sucked in a deep breath. "Which is the reason for the tears. Not the flight attendant or you thinking I didn't belong in first class. Tonight is hardly the first time someone has judged me."

There was a story there, but not one that two perfect strangers shared.

"But thank you for apologizing." She offered him a smile then turned her head toward the flight attendant as she started giving the mandatory safety instructions.

His seatmate clearly wasn't expecting any further conversation, which wasn't surprising given his initial rudeness and headphones. He typically hated flying with a chatty seat neighbor, but he wanted to know more about the woman beside him.

Maybe it was her statement about being judged; he understood that better than most. It was a driving need he couldn't explain. "I'm Kostas. Will you be away from home for long?"

Her hazel eyes studied him and she looked like she was weighing her answer. A skill he'd developed while living in the royal household, though he wondered where she might have learned it and if it was part of the judgment she'd experienced.

"Calla Lewis," she sighed, shrugging as she pulled her legs into her lap.

He was a little jealous that she could adjust her frame in the uncomfortable seat. At six feet five inches, even the legroom in first class was a tight fit.

"I took rotation assignment for a year. I'm a replacement for a woman on maternity leave." Calla pursed her lips, "Anyways…hopefully, I'll be back after that. But life—" She blew out a breath and pushed a strand of hair that had escaped her messy bun out of her eye. "Life has a way of changing any carefully made plans. At least, in my experience."

"Mine too." He laughed.

Calla let out a soft chuckle. "The best laid plans are no match for life's chaos." The plane started forward and she leaned a little closer. "Would you mind if I looked out the window? I've never left Seattle."

"Of course." Kostas wished they could switch seats now. Wished he'd not taken the easy answer of staying in place during their awkward exchange. But they couldn't switch while the plane was taking off.

She leaned across him and energy seemed to race across his skin as her light scent invaded his nose. He took a deep breath, trying to control the unusual response. He didn't react...especially to strangers.

"No way to do this without invading your personal space." Calla smiled as she glanced at him yet he could see the unshed tears in her eyes.

She was a stranger, but he'd left home before. Fled was a more accurate term. He remembered the mixture of excitement, dread and homesickness that had accompanied that first flight. "What's your favorite thing about Seattle?"

"The rain." She put her hand over her mouth as the lights of the city became smaller. Then the entire landscape disappeared below the clouds.

Calla leaned back in her seat, though she kept her body shifted toward him. "I love the rain. I know people come from elsewhere who complain that it feels like it's always raining—which it's not."

"But it happens enough to feel like it's always." Kostas grinned.

"Statistically, we get less rain than much of the US. It just happens on more days than most places."

He laughed and leaned a little closer. Discussing rain shouldn't be invigorating, but he enjoyed seeing the hint of fire in Calla's eyes. "That sounds like something only someone born in Seattle would brag about. There is moss growing on the buildings."

Calla opened her mouth but instead of defending her home city, she clicked her tongue and pointed to him. "I supposed you're headed some place sunny and warm."

"Sunnier and warmer than Seattle. But that is a low bar to climb over." He winked, answering the question, but not directly. He loved the island of Palaío, but he didn't want to talk about home. Didn't want to think of the responsibilities waiting for him.

"Is New York your final destination?"

If Calla noticed him shifting the topic away from himself, she didn't acknowledge it. Instead, she shook her head and yawned. "No. Though part of me wishes it was. It's the first stop in my four layovers. From New York to London and then on to progressively tinier airports."

"New York to Paris for me. Then on to one tiny airport and a ship."

"Adventure!" Calla smiled, but he could see the worry in her eyes as she looked toward the window. Seattle was far behind them; with the speed of the airplane, they were likely two-thirds across the state by now.

The airplane shook and Calla grabbed his hand. Her cheeks colored as she immediately pulled back. "Oh, my. Sorry. I… I have clearly never been on a plane."

His fingers ached to take her hand back. To touch her. It was such a dangerous thought. He didn't know Calla, and their paths were only passing on this one flight, but part of him felt like he should want to know her. Should want to hold her hand. It was an uncomfortable sensation, but one he didn't want to push away.

"I don't mind." He put his hand on the shared armrest and winked. "It's here in case you need it. But I hope the plane doesn't experience any real turbulence."

"Have you ever experienced that?" She twitched her nose before hitting her palm against her head. "Chalk that up as questions a nervous flier shouldn't ask their seatmate. Especially since there is no chance we will be on the same flight once we hit our destination."

She pursed her lips as she shifted in the chair. "Though even if we were on the same plane, we wouldn't be seatmates since I am very much flying coach the rest of the way. But this is nice!"

It was nice. He knew she meant the extra legroom and quick service. But he'd flown around the world since he was a small boy, and Kostas had never had such a fun experience. She let out another yawn and he knew their banter was ending.

That was the problem with red-eye flights. This one was supposed to land in New York at four in the morning. His plane left for Paris at six and he'd never see the woman next to him again.

A touch of sadness ran through him as she

covered her mouth for her third yawn in less than five minutes. He reached up and flipped off the small reading lights above them. "You should get some rest. You'll be exhausted with all the travel, but sleeping now will help with the transition. Trust me."

"Well, you seem to be a travel expert…or as close to one as I can ask now. Thanks for making me feel better, Kostas. The last year…" She paused as she looked at the window before letting her eyes wander to his in the darkened cabin. "It's been rough. Anyways…thanks, again."

"Anytime." It was a phrase so many people threw away. A conversation rejoinder that really meant nothing. But for the first time in forever, Kostas wished it truly meant that she could reach out to him anytime. That they had a connection.

Clearly, his nerves were more frayed at the thought of returning home than he wanted to admit. But at least Calla had given him a few minutes of relief.

Midwife Calla Lewis was tired, but she didn't think she could sleep. The exhaustion floating through her body refused to take over her brain's wanderings. She was really on the first leg of her twenty-four-hour-plus journey to the small island off the coast of Greece.

When she'd first talked to the recruiter for her international travel nursing program, Calla hadn't really expected it to lead anywhere. It was just one of the many options she'd explored to pay off her debt as fast as possible. But then the recruiter had let her know there was an opportunity on the small island nation of Palaío; one of their midwives was on her twelve-month maternity leave. It was a posting that came with a furnished apartment and an excellent salary to compete with the international shortage of nurses.

She'd been warned that the clinic was going through some changes. The main doctor was retiring after serving nearly sixty years, according to the recruiter, and there were only two other midwives plus a traveling OBGYN.

The island community was small, but the women deserved the safest option when they were delivering. And the king of Palaío was determined to recruit the best for his subjects with the understanding that the nurse she would be replacing planned to return from maternity leave. It was a year rotation with the opportunity to stay on, if the clinic needed it. But one year was all she needed. One year to get back on her feet.

Calla still couldn't wrap her mind around the fact that the king of Palaío was taking such a close interest in the clinic. He'd not been able to attend the interview panel that had met with her and the agency representative, yet had sent along his apologies. It was a little overwhelming.

But overwhelming didn't really matter. She owed Liam almost forty thousand dollars.

Liam.

In another world, today she was supposed to be honeymooning in Jamaica. She pinched her eyes, as if she closed them tighter the memories would float away. Her thumb wandered to the missing ring on her left finger.

It had been gone for almost a year. At first, she couldn't believe that after five years together, after planning a life, after supporting each other…after she'd done everything he'd asked of her to impress his impossible parents, he'd still chosen his family money over her. Then demanded she repay the "loan" he'd given her for her masters in midwifery program. *Loan*…

She hadn't asked him to pay off her student loan. He'd done it because his parents had already thought she wasn't good enough for their son. It had taken her three months after her broken engagement to realize that Liam had never thought she was good enough for him, either.

That stung. Not that her ex was a jerk, but that she'd let him control her. Done her best to fit the mold he'd wanted. Dyed her hair when he'd said he preferred blond, dressed the way he and his parents preferred. The only thing she hadn't done was give up her career.

And that had been the deal breaker. That was fine, but asking for repayment on what he'd called a gift was the reason she was on this plane. The reason she was traveling thousands of miles away from the only place she'd known.

The salary included room and board. With any luck and some thriftiness, she'd repay him and have her life back on track by the end of the contract.

The plane shuddered again and Calla almost reached for Kostas's hand. She wanted to, so badly. He'd offered, and she'd thought the offer was genuine, but then, it had taken her over five years to realize who Liam was. She wasn't sure she could trust her gut anymore.

Luckily, the plane stopped its tremors after a few seconds. It was just the normal bumps that, supposedly, accompanied air travel. With any luck, by the time she landed in Palaío, she'd feel like a true travel veteran. But she doubted it.

She yawned again and shifted in her seat. Her shoulder connected with Kostas's and her body heated at the simple touch. That was the thing she missed the most about being in a relationship. The little touches.

Hand-holding, hugs after a rough day, bumping another's hip at a joke, falling asleep on someone's shoulder. It had been a year since she'd shared those simple pleasures. A year of loneliness.

Still, she'd take lonely to the control she'd let Liam exercise over her. Every single day for the rest of her life, if necessary. Calla liked who she was, and she wasn't changing for someone again.

She yawned for what felt like the hundredth time since she'd stepped onto the plane, but her brain finally drifted away. She sighed as her body slowly lost its fight against exhaustion.

It didn't feel like she'd been asleep for long when the pillow under her shifted and her lopsided glasses dug into her cheek. It took a moment to realize that she didn't have a pillow and for mortification to creep up her spine as Kostas moved beside her.

Dear God. She'd fallen asleep on his shoulder. The man was gorgeous. Tall, with dark, curly hair and a five-o'clock shadow. He wore slacks and a loose shirt that screamed designer goods. A model compared to her sloppy travel gear. And she'd fallen asleep on him!

"I'm sorry to wake you. They've put out a request for a doctor." Kostas's voice was warm as he hit the button to call the flight attendant.

"No. I'm sorry. I didn't—" She stopped as the flight attendant stepped up beside them.

"Are you a medical professional?"

"I'm an obstetrician."

The response sent the final fog of sleepiness from Calla's brain as she registered the conversation.

"Oh, thank God. We've got a passenger in coach who thinks she's in labor."

Calla unbuckled her seat belt as she stated, "I'm a nurse practitioner and midwife."

The flight attendant visibly relaxed. Having any doctor onboard was a gift, but having the exact right combination of needed medical professionals was a miracle.

Kostas nodded. "You're perfect, aren't you?"

Perfect. Calla tried not to flinch at the term. Perfection was what Liam had demanded, and she'd always fallen short.

"Not really. Want me to get washed up first while you check on the patient or do you want to wash up first?" An airplane was not the best place to sanitize one's hands, and if she couldn't deliver a baby in a hospital, there were at least a dozen other locations she'd pick before an airplane thousands of miles above the earth. But you worked with what you had.

"I'll check the patient first. Hopefully, it's strong Braxton-Hicks."

Calla nodded to acknowledge she'd heard Kostas as she made her way to the bathroom. She hoped it was false contractions, but if it wasn't, they needed to be prepared.

The attendant followed her and Calla turned to ask, "Once we've washed our hands, do you have non-latex gloves in case we need to check the mother?" Less than one percent of the general population had a latex allergy, but she'd prefer not to take any additional risks.

"Yes. I'll grab them."

Calla washed up as quickly as she could professionally manage in the tiny compartment. She quickly gloved and went to find Kostas and their patient.

Stepping into coach was like stepping into a different world. The whole back of the plane was awake, and she could see a few phones out. No doubt this would be on people's social media platforms as soon as they landed. *If not before.*

She made her way to the woman sitting close to the front and noticed the small pool of liquid under the seat. *Amniotic fluid?*

Calla looked from it to Kostas and saw him nod.

"Becky, meet midwife Calla."

Then he turned to the flight attendant. "Why don't we move to first class? More room…" He nodded to the number of phones being held up. "And more privacy."

"Of course."

Kostas smiled at Becky. "Calla is going to go with you to first class and check you while I get cleaned up." Kostas's tone was soft but commanding. "Calla, this is Becky. She is thirty-three weeks pregnant with her second daughter. Contractions are steady at six minutes apart."

So this was the real deal in the air! When she'd

thought of this next step as an adventure, she hadn't meant for it to kick off with such a bang.

"My OB cleared me to travel." Becky's bottom lip trembled as Kostas guided her to first class and then helped settle her onto a blanket on the floor.

"I'm sure he did. You did nothing wrong, Becky. Nothing."

Calla wasn't sure Becky registered Kostas's words, but they were absolutely the right ones. She had done nothing wrong and preterm labor was not a punishment. It was just something that happened.

The good news was that at thirty-three weeks, Becky's daughter had an excellent chance of being able to tell this story to all her friends as a teenager.

"It's lovely to meet you, Becky. Let's get you checked, so we know how far along you are." Calla kept her tone level, trying to calm the scared mom despite the most unlikely situation.

She watched the flight attendants hold up blankets to give the women some privacy, though the other four first-class passengers were kind enough to look engrossed in their phones.

Calla smiled as she checked Becky, but she couldn't stop the shift of her face as she felt the cord in the vaginal canal. *Prolapse.*

"What?" Becky's face was white as she stared

at Calla. "And don't say it's nothing. I can tell it's not."

"You're right." Calla kept her voice steady as she gently pushed the cord up to give the baby some relief. "The umbilical cord is prolapsed, which means..."

"I know what it means. I remember from birthing class. We're on a plane. Oh, my God."

"First, I know this is hard and scary. But I need you to take a deep breath. With me." Calla breathed in and out then did it again as Becky followed her.

"Now, I am going to remove my hand. I want you to get on all fours, then put your head down on the ground."

"Puppy pose."

Calla raised an eyebrow but didn't ask as Becky moved into position.

"I'm a yoga instructor. I..." She let out a soft sob. "What now?"

"Now, I keep the cord lifted until we get you to the hospital." Calla repositioned herself and found the cord immediately.

Before she could alert the flight attendants to the situation, Kostas peeked over the blankets. He saw the position Becky was in and Calla watched as his shoulders tensed before he calmly looked at the attendants.

"We need to be on the ground. As soon as possible, with an ambulance waiting to take us to a facility capable of performing a cesarean. Alert the pilot now. This is a medical emergency."

Becky let out a sob and Kostas bent to her level. "I'm sorry, Becky. But we will get you the best possible help as soon as possible. Until then, if you feel the need to push, I need you to do your best to avoid it. Understand?"

"Yes."

Kostas turned his attention to Calla. "They are going to perform an emergency landing. It will be a quick descent and air regulations require passengers in their seats."

"We can't do that." Calla shifted her legs to brace them against the chairs on either side of her. She could feel the baby move against her hand. The little girl was still okay. If she moved or Becky sat in a chair, the cord compression could kill the child.

"I know. But they are going to ask." Kostas looked at her and she saw the same determination she felt ripping through her. Becky and her daughter were their patients now. And they'd do their utmost to make sure she got the best outcome possible.

Directing her attention to Becky, Calla asked, "Are you willing to risk staying here on the floor? I have my feet braced against the seats to keep us from sliding."

Becky reached out and grabbed the legs of the chairs beside her. "Anything for my daughter."

Calla nodded and looked at Kostas. "You need to sit and buckle in. If something happens, one of us needs to take care of Becky and her daughter."

He opened his mouth like he planned to say something, but no words escaped as he shut it and looked at the empty seat. The one where she'd fallen asleep on his shoulder...the one that was actually his. He buckled in just as the announcement started.

"Ladies and gentlemen. As many of you are aware, we have a medical emergency on board. We will land in Dayton, Ohio, in ten minutes. Flight crew, prepare for landing."

The attendants holding the blankets handed them to the passengers opposite Kostas. The man continued to hold his end up as the flight attendants began giving orders.

The plane shifted and Calla braced herself. This was going to be the longest ten minutes of her career.

"Calla." Kostas's tone was steady as she met his dark gaze. "You've got this."

She nodded, not trusting her voice to not wobble as the plane started its descent. She hoped he understood how much she appreciated the faith she heard in his voice.

They barely knew each other. Theirs was a passing connection now forever bound by a medical emergency. When the plane landed, she was going to the hospital with Becky. He was headed on to Paris.

Even if he wanted to treat Becky, he'd said he practiced in Washington, so he didn't have permission to treat patients at whatever hospital they were headed to. It hurt to know that the handsome stranger who'd let her sleep on his shoulder, who'd offered a genuine connection—the first one she'd had since before Liam's falsehoods—would disappear. It had been a balm to her soul she hadn't known she'd needed.

As soon as the plane's wheels hit the ground, she let out a soft cheer. The worst part was nearly over.

Kostas unbuckled and got down to Becky's level. "How are you doing?"

"Still…here." She let out a rough breath as another contraction took her.

He looked up at Calla and raised a brow. "And you?"

Calla offered what she hoped was a reassuring smile. "Still here."

Kostas stood and looked out the window. "I can see the ambulance."

The main door to the cabin opened and he bent for what Calla knew was the last time. She looked at him, desperate to remember his handsome features so she could recall them when she told the story in the future of the sweet and handsome physician who'd assisted her with the most trying delivery of her career. His dark eyes sparkled and there were a few freckles along his nose. It would have to be enough.

"Good luck, Becky."

"Thank you."

"It was nice to meet you, Kostas." Calla hoped the few words contained all the emotions she was feeling.

"It was nice to meet you, too, Calla. Good luck on your assignment."

"Good luck at home. I hope it isn't as stressful as you fear." She offered him a smile as the EMTs stepped up behind him.

Kostas nodded as he turned to tell the medics what was going on. Then he faded into the background of the plane's chaos.

She was sad to see him go. There were other things to focus on, but a part of her felt bereft at the idea that she'd never see him again.

CHAPTER TWO

CALLA TRIED TO cover the yawn as she looked in on Becky and her daughter. While the race to the hospital in Dayton had felt like it had taken forever, from the time the plane landed to when the doctors at Miami Valley Hospital had brought Becky's little one into the world, it had been less than forty minutes. An impressive feat.

And now that the adrenaline was wearing off, Calla was dead on her feet and suddenly very aware that all her belongings, including her purse, with a way to pay for her to get back to the airport were…

Well, they were somewhere. Calla did not know where. That was a problem for after she said goodbye to Becky.

Her daughter was stable and breathing without extra oxygen. She was a little bigger than the average thirty-three-week infant. A great sign.

Becky and her newborn would be here in the hospital for a few days at least, but their prognosis was excellent.

She knocked on the door and entered when she heard the soft call from the other side.

"Calla." Becky's eyes held that tired but blissful look that all new moms shared after delivery. "I can't thank you enough. Without you…"

Becky's eyes filled with tears and Calla moved to her side. The combination of the last several hours of stress, giving birth, and the hormones that elevated then dropped following birth were enough to unseat anyone. "Everything is fine. And I am so glad that Kostas and I were there."

Kostas…

The name on her lips made her breath stop. She'd known the man for less than four hours and spoken to him for less than twenty minutes. His dark brown eyes, with flecks of gold around the edges, shouldn't be so easy to recall.

It should be a passing connection. *It was a passing connection.*

"I will always be thankful that you were there. And…" She offered a watery smile. "My daughter, Caroline Calla, will know about the nurse who saved her."

There was no way to express the emotions pouring through Calla. It was such a sweet tribute. She squeezed Becky's hand. "Thank you." The words were soft, but she hoped Becky knew how much the honor meant.

"My husband is on his way." Becky looked

at her phone. "He started calling for flights the second we landed."

It was great that Becky's husband was en route. "How did he know?" Calla hadn't meant for the question to slip out. Maybe a medic had asked while she'd focused on making sure the umbilical cord didn't compress.

"Kostas." Becky let out a soft chuckle. "No idea how, but he called Mitch, and I'm too tired to worry about the how."

Calla took that as her cue. "You should get some rest. Congratulations on your little girl. I wish you a lifetime of happiness and love." She headed for the door before Becky could argue. She needed her rest.

How did Kostas reach him? The thought niggled in the back of her brain. Airlines were known for their rigid rules and privacy concerns. However he'd done it, it was sweet.

His dark eyes flashed in her memory, *again*, as she moved down the hallway and Calla mentally shook herself. She needed to find a way to the airport and hoped all her things hadn't flown on to London without her. Even her cell phone was in her backpack, which she'd also left behind on the plane.

Pushing open the waiting room doors, her feet stopped in their path. Kostas sat in one of the most uncomfortable-looking chairs she'd ever seen. "What?" The word echoed in the room as he smiled at her and stood.

It was then that she noticed her luggage at his feet. Her lip trembled as she saw the old sec-ondhand suitcases her parents had purchased at a thrift store almost twenty years ago. Ugly but functional was the best description, and she'd never been happier to see the faded green bags in her life.

Kostas handed her the backpack she'd left on the plane. "Figured life would be easier if you had these things."

"Thank you," she whispered as she looked at her things. "But your flight home?"

He shrugged. "There will be other flights. I let my family know about the delay. My brother is disappointed, but that is nothing new."

"Kostas." She laid her hand over his, reflexive.

He squeezed her hand as he added, "I fly out tomorrow morning. Paris to Italy to…" He hesi-tated for a moment before finishing. "To home."

The hesitation struck her. She was an only child, and her family had loved her uncondi-tionally. If her parents were still alive, they'd celebrate her return home, no matter the circum-stances. She hated that not everyone had had the same experience.

Growing up, her parents were the ones ev-eryone wanted. The ones cheering at her soc-cer games, never missing a band concert, and clearly infatuated with each other. Losing them to cancer within a year of each other had nearly destroyed her.

But she knew she'd been lucky. To have seen their love, to know it was possible. So many of her friends went home to a house that lacked love…or worse.

Liam's parents had controlled every aspect of their son's life. The sports he'd participated in, the schools he'd attended, even his degree in engineering had been mandated by his father.

And the woman he'd married last weekend had been their choice too.

He'd had a chance to leave that life. Their life together would have been less privileged than he'd known, but she'd believed love could overcome that. Except he hadn't loved her…not really. And she would never settle for less again.

She didn't know Kostas's story, but a man who sat for hours in a hospital waiting room with a practical stranger's luggage was someone she wanted to know. He called to her in a way no one had before.

And he was attractive…actually, he was hot with multiple T's. The man looked like he belonged on billboards; his curly hair dipped over his ears and his shadowed beard gave him a rugged look that would make anyone's mouth water. His dark eyes seemed to see straight to her soul.

Kostas's looks were enough to make her want

to dream of kissing him. His thoughtfulness, his compassionate spirit, made her want to follow through with the action. Shame they were basically two ships passing in the night.

He squeezed her hand. He leaned close and, for a moment, she thought about what might happen if she lifted her lips and grazed his cheeks.

Kostas held her gaze, the energy between them crackling, then he dropped her hand and reached into his pocket. "You need to call this number to reschedule your flights. I rented a car, so if you can get out today, I can get you to the airport."

"And if I can't get out until tomorrow?" Calla looked at him and saw the corners of his lips tilt up. It was as forward as she'd ever been. But she wanted to spend the day with him, wanted a memory to keep her warm during the lonely nights to come in Palaío.

"Then we'll have to grab something to eat and see what we can do to keep ourselves occupied until we head out." His mouth broke into a full smile then, and her body heated at the desire pooling in his eyes.

A day with the man before her was the perfect way to start her adventure.

Kostas grinned as he watched Calla step to the side and call the number he'd given her.

Unbeknownst to her, he'd spoken with the airline and made sure they'd upgraded her to first class for her entire trip. The customer service rep had refused to give him her itinerary, which he understood, but had accepted his credit card number and put it in Calla's file, agreeing to just call it an upgrade for the service she'd provided Becky.

Calla had earned the pampering and extra space on her long trip. If the luggage and worn backpack at his side were any indicators, she rarely got pampered. And she'd more than earned it. He also knew that there were generally open seats in first class on overseas flights in the current economy. That meant it was possible he'd take her to the airport as soon as she hung up the phone.

His brother's secretary had taken the news of his delay with more grace than he figured Ioannis would. Significantly more than his father would have. But his delay couldn't be helped.

Mostly...

Kostas could have stayed on the fight with the other passengers. If he had, he'd be on his way to Paris now. But he wouldn't trade the look on Calla's face when she'd seen him in the waiting room for anything.

He wanted more time with the nurse who'd fallen asleep on his shoulder, risked her safety during landing, and hadn't even asked the flight attendants to grab her backpack as the EMTs had loaded her and Becky into the ambulance. The woman had touched a part of him that had been dormant for so long.

Kostas kept to himself. The few women he'd dated in Seattle always complained that he held them at arm's length. Complaints he understood. But how to explain that it was for their own good?

That the life of a royal bride was far from the fairy-tale ending. That your life was never truly your own. A gilded cage was still a cage.

Living in the States had given him more freedom than he'd had in Palaío, but it hadn't changed who he was. Dr. Kostas Drakos was the title he'd earned, the one he loved. But it didn't replace the title of prince of Palaío. Didn't strip away the responsibilities he was returning to.

It was easier to remain single. Besides, no woman had made him want to challenge that thought.

Calla… His heart rate picked up as she put her phone back in her pocket. Calla intrigued him. He'd wanted to see her again. Wanted to spend more than the few hours they'd had on the red-eye together—hours that had been cut painfully short.

This wasn't a forever love story. But for a few hours, he could pretend that the woman who touched his heart, who seemed to understand his hesitation to return home, might be someone special. Then they'd get on separate flights and he'd go back to being Prince Kostas once more.

"So I can't get out until tomorrow morning, either."

"Are we on the same flight to New York?" Kostas couldn't keep the grin from his face. If she wasn't sitting next to him on the plane, he could ask someone to switch seats with them. A few extra hours.

The frown appearing on her lips twisted his stomach.

"I'm not going through New York now. The quickest way to get me to my final destination is through Charlotte. I'll be a day late. I let my contact know and they understand, but…"

"But nothing." Kostas reached for her hand and squeezed it. "You need to get where you're going." Her stomach growled and he quirked a brow. "Sounds like we need to find sustenance."

"Not hospital food." She bit her lip as he laughed.

"Of course not! I don't know what we might find in Dayton, but I figure we can find something better than the hospital cafeteria."

He grabbed her ancient luggage as she put her backpack on. "What sounds good?"

"Anything!" Her grin sent a wave of happiness through him. "I am not picky…particularly when I am hungry."

The small diner boasting the best burgers in town hummed with conversation as Calla dipped a fry in ketchup. "So, Kostas…where did you work in Seattle? I was at Regional Midwives. Mostly home births, but I was in and out of Seattle General a few times. Never saw you."

The word *did* in her sentence sent a chill down his spine. Kostas didn't like to think of his time in Seattle as over. He'd promised Ioannis he'd run the clinic in Palaío for a while and recruit a few more staff. Ioannis believed he was staying, but that wasn't Kostas's plan. Still, he couldn't ask his administrator to keep him on staff while he was gone. So he'd turned in his resignation. Hating the decision, even though he'd known it was the right one.

"I had admitting privileges at Seattle General, but saw most of my patients at Grace Hospital."

"Ah." Calla dipped another fry, and he watched as she ate what was more ketchup than fry before putting more of the condiment on her plate.

She saw his gaze and laughed. "My parents always said I could just eat straight ketchup, but I don't."

He chuckled and shrugged. He'd never gotten much into the tomato-based condiment, but if it made her happy, Kostas didn't care. "I prefer mustard."

"On fries?"

He nodded, enjoying the look of horror cross her face.

She playfully shuddered as she held up another red-covered fry. "Bite your tongue!"

He laughed and held up both hands. "It's good. Promise."

"I am going to take your word for it…and ignore it." She winked and her knee pressed against his. It had happened a few times in the tight booth, and she'd moved it away each time. This time, she left it.

The small connection sent heat pouring through him as her hazel gaze held him. Then she yawned, and he couldn't keep the yawn from his lips, either.

"You're exhausted." Calla smiled as she dipped her final fry.

"You yawned first." Kostas tapped her leg with his, enjoying the pink rising in her cheeks. She was lovely.

Calla waved to the waitress and asked for the check. When Kostas made for his wallet, she held up her hand. "You brought my luggage, sat and waited for me, and somehow convinced the airline to upgrade me for the rest of my trip. I got this."

He started to argue then held his tongue. Her eyes blazed with seriousness. She wanted to pay. He could force the issue, by why take away something that was important to her? So he reached for her free hand as she put the money on the table and told the waitress that she didn't need change.

Calla looked at his hand in hers and the pink invaded her cheeks again as he ran a thumb along her palm. The easiness between them was something he'd never experienced. Maybe because there was no agenda between them. They each understood that whatever this was, it had an expiration date.

The clock would strike tomorrow morning. His heart clenched as he thought of that. He didn't want to think of the eventual goodbye. But she was also exhausted, and he was nearly dead on his feet.

It was barely three o'clock local time, but now that they had full bellies, they were each fighting the fatigue. A fight they were destined to lose.

"I have a hotel room." Her eyes popped open as he raced on. "It's the penthouse suite, so it has two full bedrooms." He wanted her, craved knowing what her lips felt like, how she tasted, but he'd never force his advances.

Calla looked at their fingers entwined, as if they'd known each other for days or weeks rather than hours.

"And if I didn't want to stay in the extra room?"

Before he could answer, she let out another yawn. As much as he wanted to follow the thread she was also clearly interested in, they were both too tired to really enjoy it. "You're free to sleep wherever you want. But I think we both need a hot shower and a few hours' rest. Then we can see where the rest of the time goes. Fair?"

"Fair," Calla agreed as she bit back another yawn.

As the hot water streamed over her, Calla tried to gather her thoughts. She was in the penthouse of a luxury hotel, in a bathroom that was bigger than her Seattle apartment. It was a little unnerving.

She felt like a fish out of water, except she was enjoying the experience. Far too much, maybe. Calla had never gone to bed with a man she barely knew. Never even considered it. But something about Kostas called to her.

In fiction, this would be the soul-mate moment, the fate of mates destined for each other. Instant connections happened, but they were mostly rooted in lust. And she certainly lusted after the man.

Her nipples were hard as she pulled the towel around herself. Kostas was showering in the other bathroom. *A hotel room with two full-sized bathrooms.* Even when she was with Liam, they'd never stayed in a place like this.

Yet Kostas didn't seem concerned with helping her, didn't seem to mind the very apparent differences in their bank accounts. He seemed to just like being around her. That was intoxicating. She dropped a long shirt over herself and stepped into the room.

Kostas was already lying on the bed. He set his tablet down. He was shirtless, but had on a pair of comfortable-looking blue jeans. Her mouth watered at the sight of his chiseled chest. Man, he was gorgeous.

Part of her wished she'd stepped out in some lacy nightgown. A ridiculous thought given their short acquaintance—and the fact that she didn't have any fancy nightgowns.

Nerves cascaded around her body as she stepped to the bed. Kostas smiled and she nearly melted. But he didn't rush her, clearly realizing that part of her was still uncertain.

"Calla…"

Her name on his lips made her decision. She wanted to lie next to him. Wanted him. She slid into his arms, enjoying the feel of his warm skin against hers. Before he could say anything else, Calla pressed her lips to his.

Kostas's grip tightened as she opened her mouth. His tongue darted across hers and she sighed. This felt right. It was a fantasy; she knew that. But a fantasy that felt so perfect.

She deepened the kiss, willing the yawn she felt building in the back of her throat away. She had a lifetime to rest; she had less than fifteen hours with Kostas, and she wanted to make them last.

"You're tired." Kostas broke the kiss, his fingers tracing along her side as if he couldn't keep from touching her.

"So are you." She dropped a kiss at his lips. "I don't care." It was the truth. She didn't want to miss whatever chemistry was driving them. Calla could sleep on the plane tomorrow, but something in her screamed that if she missed this opportunity, if she missed being with him, she'd regret it for the rest of her life.

Calla kissed him again then pulled back. "But if you need sleep…"

He pursed his lips as he stared at her. "I need you." The words sounded primal as they escaped his lips, his eyes dilated with passion.

His hands slipped up the shirt she was wearing and found her nipples. He ran his thumbs across them as he kissed her again. Each touch sent flickers of flames along her skin as he explored her.

Kostas let out a guttural noise as her lips trailed his neck and she smiled against him, loving his reaction. He lifted the shirt over her head and leaned back, studying her.

Maybe she should feel self-conscious. But the shame or nervousness she thought she'd feel if she ever fell into bed with a man she'd just met failed to appear. Her body longed for his touch, craved it. That was a gift she refused to push away.

"You are so lovely." His deep voice covered

her as his hand slid to the top of her thigh. "So very lovely."

"You already said that." She let out a sigh as his mouth trailed along her stomach.

"It bears repeating." His lips caressed her nipples, suckling each one with a gentleness that consumed her.

"Kostas…"

His fingers dragged across her inner thigh, so close to where she wanted him. *Needed him.*

She felt him smile against her chest as he stroked her nipple with his tongue before drifting down her body. His motions were slow, achingly slow. And she loved each touch.

He reached her belly button and then moved back to her nipples, lingering as she sucked in a deep breath. Kostas's fingers feathered her body; sketches that varied from the lightest brush to a touch that felt like he was barely holding back from claiming her.

His tongue traced her as he finally meandered down her body again. His fingers teasing as he trailed so close to her sex. "Kostas…"

"I enjoy the sound of my name on your lips, Calla." His thumb pressed against her bud and she let out a cry, arching her back as her body exploded. "It may be the most perfect sound. Look at me, sweetheart."

She opened her eyes, quivering as his fingers pressed into her. He smiled as he touched her, grinning as he watched her enjoy the scorching pleasure he was bringing her. It was thrilling.

His thumb pressed against her as his fingers stroked her. "Calla."

Her name dripping from his lips as he pleasured her sent her over the edge again.

"Kostas…" She was breathless. She should feel sated after the two breathtaking orgasms, but she wanted more. Needed more.

"I need you."

He dropped his lips to hers, but she grabbed either side of his face, halting his attentions. "I want you…all of you. Now."

Only after getting her demand out did she join their mouths, loving the taste of him as she reached between them and undid the button of his jeans. Unzipping him, she slid her hand in, finding what she craved most.

"Calla." He whispered her name as he stripped his jeans off. He pulled a condom from the back pocket, and she reached for it.

Holding his smoky gaze, she opened it, sheathing him. Then she straddled him, watching his lips part as she eased her way slowly down his length.

His hands gripped her hips, but he didn't rush her.

He spent forever driving her closer and closer to the edge before finally giving her what she needed. She planned to repay the favor in the most delicious way possible.

Kostas's eyes held hers as she gently rocked their bodies, refusing to yield to her body's demand to move faster. She wanted to savor every moment.

His fingers drifted to her nipples again, swirling them in perfect symphony with her movements. They melded together, and everything else seemed to disappear. Kostas sat up and she wrapped her legs around him as he kissed her.

The sensations were almost too much. She let out a groan and finally gave in to the heady needs claiming them both. When she came for a final time, it was with Kostas's name on her lips.

Calla's soft snores echoed in the dark room as Kostas pulled her into his arms. Their alarms would go off in less than an hour. And in less than four, they'd be on different planes, their paths forever moving in different directions. And he hated the thought.

It wasn't fair to want more from her. Particularly when he knew he couldn't bring her to Palaío. On the island, the man he was, the man he wanted to be, transformed into a prince. And this time he was determined to kill the "rebel son" label he'd earned as an angry teen. Now he'd be the man the kingdom needed, a skilled doctor, but cold, distant, always ensuring he followed protocols.

He'd fled after what had happened with Maria. After his father had refused to refute the ugly and untrue rumors. He was a grown adult now, and he would not let lies stand. But for the next year or so, he doubted there be much news for the press to latch onto. He had a role to play, expectations to fulfill. And he'd be perfect.

Perfect!

That didn't mean he didn't want to beg Calla to visit him. To want to show her the crystal-clear water as it lapped onto the beaches. Needed to show her all the places special to him.

It was beyond selfish. If she landed in Palaío and the press saw the connection between them, they'd make her life a living hell. She'd grow to resent him, just as Maria had.

It stung when Maria had fled, but he'd understood.

He barely knew Calla, but he suspected seeing disappointment grow in her eyes would be just as bad. *Maybe worse.*

This day, this one twenty-four-hour period, would have to sate his desires for the rest of time. He let his fingers trail along her delicate body, enjoying the little sighs escaping her lips. She was so beautiful.

He dropped his lips to the base of her neck, right where her shoulder and neck met. The place where, when he'd trailed his lips along it last night, she'd cried out his name.

Kostas lightly stroked her hip. Her skin was so soft under his fingers. He wanted to memorize how she felt, how she tasted, how perfectly she fit with him. He let his hand travel to her breasts, running a finger along her nipple, smiling as he felt it harden.

She rolled over in his hold, her eyes meeting his in the room's dim lights. Her lips traced his chin as her hand moved south. "Can I help you, Kostas?"

He didn't bother to mince words, didn't want to hide the need he felt. "I want you, Calla. So badly."

She ginned as she kissed him. "The feeling is very mutual."

He gripped her and rolled with her, losing himself in the sensations that were simply Calla.

CHAPTER THREE

CALLA WALKED ALONG the beach in Palaío, holding herself tightly as she watched the sun rise along the edge of the ocean. She'd been on the island nation for less than seventy-two hours, and most of those she'd spent sleeping.

And dreaming of Kostas.

Their parting at the airport had been the stuff of movies. The tragic ones that people sat on their couches clutching tissues, waiting for the inevitable relief that tears brought. And she'd replayed it repeatedly in her head.

He'd stayed with her until she'd boarded her flight to London. His hand clasping hers. For a moment, she'd pretended he was coming with her. It was only when she sank into her plush first-class seat alone that she'd let the emotion of their last kiss at the gate float through her.

She'd spent most of the trip trying to keep her weepiness in check. It was ridiculous to cry over a one-night stand. A beautiful one-night stand. A memory she'd cherish forever, though one might think she'd left her soul mate in Dayton. It was ridiculous, but part of her had wanted to run back down the ramp, jump into his arms and tell him she wanted to see if the connection between them was more than lust.

But she had a job in Palaío. The income would let her cut the final ties to her past. Getting on the flight to Palaío had been the right move.

Calla blew out a breath as the waves crashed close to her feet. She'd done the right thing. That didn't mean that she didn't wish another option had been available.

She started at the Palaío Women's Clinic today. She was still kicking the last of her jet lag, but Calla didn't care. Once she was at the clinic, the work would take prime focus in her mind. She loved working as a midwife. It consumed her.

Then she could let the memory of Kostas, the thoughts of his kisses and touches, slip to the back of her memory. Calla heard her scoff echo in the early morning light and hugged herself even tighter.

At the very least, the memory couldn't occupy all her thoughts while she was working.

She picked up a shell, fingering the ridges as she let out a breath. Squeezing the shell tightly, she brought Kostas's face into her memory. Calla let her mind trace his high cheekbones, the five-o'clock shadow he wore so perfectly, and the dark eyes that saw her so clearly.

"Goodbye, Kostas." She raised the shell above her head, getting ready to throw it. A silly ritual she'd schemed up when she'd tossed and turned in her bed last night. But her hand refused to let go.

Pathetic, Calla. Pathetic.

She wrapped her hand around the shell. In a few days, she could complete the ritual. But for now, she turned to head back to the apartment the clinic had secured for her. It was lovely, larger than her place in Seattle, and furnished with furniture nicer than she'd ever had. Palaío was great, and if she hadn't met Kostas, her heart would be happier than she'd ever been.

But she had met him.

Another soul walked the beach, and her breath caught in her throat. He walked like Kostas, carried himself in the same, almost regal, way he had. Her throat closed as she watched the man, her heart urging her to run toward him.

Luckily, she still had some of her senses. The odds of it being Kostas were so minuscule she refused to even calculate them. If she ran to the stranger, she'd be disappointed when it wasn't the man she craved.

And he'd likely be terrified of a stranger racing at him in the early morning. She looked at the man in the distance once more then purposefully started back for her apartment without looking back.

* * *

Kostas let the wet sand sink between his toes as he stared at the departing woman further up the beach. For a minute, he'd wondered if it was Calla. In the distance, with the morning's shadows, it had been too easy to pretend it might be her. He pushed a hand through his much shorter hair and turned to look out at the ocean.

He was in Palaío. Had been for almost three days, and the casing of Prince Kostas, second in line to the throne, had wrapped around him as soon as he'd stepped into the palace. He'd cut his hair after multiple comments from his brother's advisers.

Kostas wished he'd stood up to them. Explained that having the loose curls falling around his ears looked no less professional than the close cut worn by his brother. But he hadn't wanted to argue.

If the advisers thought it best that he have short hair…well, he could grow it out again as soon as he left. He'd wear the mask of Prince Kostas, the reformed rebel. That was all.

Besides, all he'd wanted to do since landing was to think of the woman he'd kissed goodbye at the airport. Nothing seemed to matter much. He was mourning a relationship that had never been.

But could have been.

He shook his head as he stepped into the ocean, letting the waves wrap around his ankles.

It was silly to keep replaying their last kiss. Silly to wish he'd asked for her email or phone number. They were on different paths, but he'd spent most of the last few days looking for her. Thinking he might see her in the street or on the beach.

His mind was intent on conjuring her. He heard a noise behind him and turned to see a photographer with a long lens above the dune. He turned back to the waves as the truth of his position weighed on him.

Even if Calla was in Palaío, which he knew she wasn't, it wouldn't matter. Here, he wasn't her Kostas. Wasn't the man who'd cradled her in sleep. On this island, he was Prince Kostas.

He shook his head. Today was a new day, and he needed to focus on his role at the clinic. It was his first day…and the new midwife's first day, too. When he'd heard that, he'd nearly screamed for Natalia to tell him the name, his mind wrapping around the possibility that he and Calla might have taken very different routes to the same place.

His personal assistant had nearly jumped away from his outburst. Then she'd apologized profusely for not knowing the information. She'd promised to get it, but Kostas had waved her off, expressing regret for his outburst. Besides, he'd find out everything about the midwife when he arrived.

His watch beeped and he closed his eyes as

he faced the rising sun. Today started his countdown. Maybe when he left, he'd see if he could locate Calla.

How?

That question had hovered around him for days. He knew her name was Calla Lewis. But he knew nothing else. He hadn't memorized the address on her baggage tags—a mistake he'd castigated himself for most of his trip to Paris.

He knew how she kissed, how her skin felt against his, but there was no way to trace her from those notes.

"Goodbye, Calla." The whispered words carried across the sand and he turned. He needed to focus on his actual mission. Do what the island needed…and then get off it. For good this time.

"I hope those photographers aren't planning on camping outside the clinic every day," Alexa muttered as she leaned against the desk in the small office where she and Calla were waiting for the new OBGYN to arrive.

"Why are they here?" Calla looked over the charting tablet the nurse practitioner had handed her when she'd walked in.

Alexa had smiled when Calla had arrived almost an hour before her shift. Calla had claimed it was because she'd wanted to organize herself, to get to know the clinic and procedures before their patients arrived. But she'd been going a little stir crazy in her apartment. Looking over the patient records, figuring out her schedule was calming.

And it lets me think of something other than Kostas.

There'd been a photographer sitting in a car when she'd first arrived, and more had appeared in the last hour. In Seattle, she'd occasionally seen journalists and photographers at the hospital, but never near the maternity wing, and usually only after a terrible accident.

"Waiting for our new OB." Alexa let out a sigh as she looked out the window. "A few of them camped out back there, too. Guess they want to make sure they covered all potential entrances."

"Did he work as a movie star at some point?" Calla chuckled as she looked up. The nurse's stare cut the sound out of her throat. "Seriously, he was in the movies?"

"No." Alexa looked at her and crossed her arms. "Did they really not tell you that you'd be working with King Ioannis's little brother? Prince Kostas?"

"Kostas?" Her throat went dry as she processed the name. No way her Kostas was a prince. He would have said something...right?

Uncertainty pooled through her. Would he have told her? Their physical connection had been deep, electric, magical, but they'd not actually spoken of where they were going.

She'd called this an adventure and he'd only said he was going home. *And that he wasn't looking forward to his family's expectations...*

No. That didn't mean anything. Far too many people had family expectations that were overburdening.

She and Kostas hadn't shared too much, but that was a protective measure, one to guard their hearts as the heat between them burned but didn't allow for any future. At least, that was how Calla viewed it and had assumed it was the same for him.

But what if was something else?

It had taken Liam almost a year before he'd told her how much wealth his family had. He'd claimed other girlfriends had used him for his family's money.

She chewed on her lower lip. Surely, her Kostas, the man she'd spent the most passionate day of her life with, wasn't a prince. It was just a name.

"If he looks half as good as he did at his brother's coronation, then he could be in the movies. But Palaío's Prodigal Prince chose medicine." The tinge of annoyance at the words *Prodigal Prince* sounded almost maternal. As if Alexa understood the desire but couldn't quite countenance the choice the royal had made.

"Where was he working before?"

"Some city in the US. Starts with sea..." Alexa tapped her finger against her chin. "Sea—"

"Seattle." Calla set the tablet down as she leaned against the desk.

"That's it!" Alexa stated.

Kostas. Her mouth was dry. Kostas *was* here. Her heart hammered as she tried to figure out what this meant. *Does it mean anything?*

They'd had one blissful night together. But they'd given in to passion because they'd never expected to see one another again—or at least that was why she'd followed her needs.

Her cheeks heated as the memory of his fingers on her skin lit up her mind.

"I said leave. This is a medical clinic, and the patients don't need cameras in their faces. They need support for their babies!"

His voice carried across the clinic and Alexa left the office. Calla couldn't seem to get her feet to move. She'd dreamed of reuniting with him since she'd kissed him goodbye in Dayton. But she'd never expected to fulfill the fantasy.

Certainly not in Palaío or after discovering he was a prince. This was the stuff of TV movies, not real life.

"Prince Kostas. It's so nice to see you." Alexa's tone was cordial, deferential, as it drifted to the office.

How was she supposed to address royalty? Particularly royalty she'd clung to? Naked.

"Dr. Drakos or Kostas will be fine, Alexa. And please don't bow. I'm second in line to the throne and soon to be third when my sister-in-law delivers. I don't want our patients uncomfortable. In this clinic, I am Dr. Kostas Drakos, nothing more."

He cleared his throat and added, "When does the new nurse midwife arrive?"

"She's already here. Calla?"

She could hear Alexa turn; no doubt surprised she hadn't followed her to greet the doctor. *The Prince.*

Calla grabbed the tablet chart and raced around the desk. "Here. Sorry, I just…" Her eyes met Kostas's and her heart cried out to go to him. He looked tired. He'd taken several planes to get here, just as she had. But the exhaustion clinging to him looked like it went deeper. The curls he'd worn so well were gone; the short hair looked regal.

But it didn't suit him.

Kostas stared at her, clearly as surprised by her appearance as she was by his. The air in the room felt thick as she dragged it in. What was she supposed to do?

Alexa cleared her throat and Kostas broke the connection with her.

"I just realized that Calla worked in Seattle, too. Did you two work together?"

"No." His voice was tight as he shook his head.

"We've never worked together. It's a huge city. There are several major hospitals in Seattle. It's a big place. It's nice to meet you, Calla."

She blinked as she registered his words. They didn't have to acknowledge the exact nature of their acquaintance, but to just dismiss her, to act like she was a complete stranger… The warmth in his eyes that she'd fallen for was gone.

The prince stood here now. In Seattle, or Dayton, she was good enough for a night. But here, in his home, she was a stranger.

Liam hadn't considered her good enough, either.

Liam had been wrong, but Kostas was actual royalty. Her throat tightened, but she refused to let him see how much his words cut. She pushed the pain radiating through her down. She'd deal with it tonight…alone.

If he wanted to act like they didn't know each other, fine. She could follow that script. "It's nice to meet you, too, Prince Kostas."

"I prefer Kostas." He looked at her, his features softening for just a moment.

She knew that. Had heard him correct Alexa. But she was using his title for herself. A reminder to Calla Lewis that she'd spent the past few days yearning for a man who considered her beneath him. A man who wouldn't even acknowledge that they'd known each other.

Hell, they could have even shared the story

of helping Becky when she'd gone into labor thirty-thousand feet above the earth. There were so many ways he could have handled it besides this one. Ways to acknowledge her.

But if he didn't want to. Well, fine!

"I look forward to working with you, Dr. Drakos." Calla kept her tone even, not trusting herself to say any more.

He opened his mouth but shut it quickly. Whatever he'd planned to say evaporating as she nodded. "I need to see to a few things in the office, before my first patient arrives."

He walked past her without another glance. Alexa followed, chattering about the day's schedule, the patients and island gossip.

Kostas met Calla's gaze briefly before he closed the office door, but he didn't smile, didn't show any reaction to her presence at all.

Calla raised her chin and closed her eyes. She'd mourned her relationship with Liam. Nursed the heartache for months before realizing it was her she was missing. The woman she'd been before she'd tried to fit into his mold.

As soon as she'd reclaimed her true self, Calla's heart had stitched itself back together. She'd sworn that she'd never change herself for another again. Never let someone have that much control over her.

Her escapade with Kostas was a fun memory. But she would not chase a man who didn't want her. Wouldn't acknowledge a prince who greeted a lover with no kindness.

She was in Palaío for a reason that had nothing to do with Prince Kostas Drakos. And she wasn't leaving, so she hoped His Royal Highness didn't expect her to wilt under his controlled gaze.

Kostas wanted to tell Alexa that he didn't care about island gossip. That he didn't know the woman she was gossiping about and didn't care that she'd married her best friend's nephew. Or that she was pregnant. When she arrived at his clinic, he'd treat her just like any other patient.

This was one of the many aspects of the life on Palaío that he hadn't missed. The country was home to a little over one hundred thousand people. Each of the island's towns, even the capital where they were, operated as small towns. Everyone still knew everyone's business, particularly the scandals. *Or perceived scandals.*

The city of Seattle had over seven times the island's population, and twenty times the capital city's population. There, it was easy to get lost in the daily hustle. Easy to only see his patients in the office. If he occasionally passed them at the grocery store or Starbucks, he'd wave, say a few pleasantries and then move on.

For the first time in his life, Kostas had been nearly invisible. Able to be just the man he wanted, without the trappings of a title. That

Kostas could have taken Calla on a date without worrying about photos and rumors and… He inhaled and discarded the thoughts. He wasn't that Kostas—no matter how much he wished for it.

"Do you mind giving me a few minutes to look over the records here alone?" Kostas saw Alexa glance at her watch as he cut off her story in midsentence then look up at him.

She nodded and headed for the door. "It's nice to have you home, Your Highness."

Before he could comment on her use of the honorific, the nurse disappeared. Calla walked by the open office door, but she didn't stop or look at him. Not that he could blame her.

His body had ignited the moment he'd seen her. Only Alexa's presence had stilled his movements. When she'd asked if they knew each other, he'd seen the hint of excitement glowing in Alexa's eyes. She'd wanted to hear the word *yes*. Wanted to deconstruct its meaning, pass it along to her friends that not only had Prince Kostas returned to Palaío, but he knew the nurse from Seattle, too.

The rumor mill would spin out of control. So he'd lied. And he'd seen the hurt in Calla's eyes. Seen her swallow so many words. Then she'd called him "Prince Kostas," and he was almost certain she'd done it intentionally.

He just wasn't sure why.

Rolling his neck, he wrapped the need crawling through him and forced it into the mental compartment he'd carefully constructed following the disasters with his mother and Maria. The photographers had followed him from the airport to the palace to the office. Hopefully, in a few days, they'd get so bored by his activities that they'd disappear.

But if word leaked that he was interested in Calla... That he'd spent the night with her... The gathering outside would look like nothing compared to the frenzy they'd experience. He couldn't do that to her.

Wouldn't.

Better to cause her hurt now than to subject her to weeks and months under the microscope. Even if part of him wanted her to join him, wanted to see if she might not mind the invasion to her life. That was the selfish inner voice that he'd learned to ignore years ago—though it surprised him how much he wanted to give in to the urge now.

"Yes, I am glowing! Look at my bump. You'd think I was having twins. Which maybe I am!"

Kostas pulled on his face as his sister-in-law's voice carried into the office. He knew Eleni didn't have an appointment this morning. So what was she doing here?

Checking on him. He sighed as he stepped into the waiting area.

Her eyes met his as she cradled her bump. "Twins." Eleni let out a chuckle. "That story ought to keep them busy for at least a few days." She looked lovely and, at eight months pregnant, she did not look like she was carrying twins.

"You don't have an appointment, Eleni." Kostas raised an eyebrow as he leaned against the door to the office. He'd looked over his list of patients last night, and Eleni was not on it.

Though the queen had a habit of doing as she liked, much to the chagrin of her security detail, she kept a much looser schedule than Kostas or Ioannis. Besides formal functions, her daily schedule was more general ideas than actual appointments. Particularly now. She'd started her maternity leave when she'd entered her third trimester and only had a handful of royal appointments.

"Not with you!" She grinned as she turned and waved. "I assume you're the new midwife?"

"I am. Calla Lewis, Your Majesty. Right on time for your appointment."

"Oh, pish! Call me Eleni, please. There is no need to be formal. I've heard so much about you from Ioannis. He was thrilled when you accepted the position. He thought you and Kostas would work well together."

Color crept up Calla's neck as she cleared her throat. "I suppose we'll find our way. If you'll follow me…"

Eleni looked to Kostas, her dark eyes laying into him before she followed Calla. There was little that got past his sister-in-law. She'd undoubtedly seen Calla blush, but being around royals often made people uncomfortable. Hopefully, Eleni would accept that answer if she pressed him on it later.

It was a minor problem for later, but Kostas followed behind them. He wanted—needed—to be near Calla.

"Do you need something, Doctor?" Calla raised her chin, challenging him at the door. "I promise you, I am more than capable of taking care of your sister-in-law."

She was right, of course. There was no need for him to follow them. Calla was perfectly capable of doing Eleni's check. At thirty-three weeks along, he knew his sister-in-law had been coming in regularly. And doing so before the other patients arrived granted her at least a little privacy.

Assuming the photographers outside left.

"I like her!" Eleni winked at Kostas. "Everyone here treats you like a prince, or a little brother. No one just stands up to you."

"You always have." Kostas crossed his arms and let his eyes wander to Calla for an instant before redirecting his attention to his sister-in-law.

"I'm different. I'm family." Eleni slid onto the table and waved to the heart monitor sitting on the counter. "I don't care if he stays, but I would like to hear my baby's heartbeat."

Calla grabbed the wand and turned all her

attention to Eleni, ignoring Kostas completely. "Are you having a boy or a girl?"

"We haven't found out." Eleni grinned as the heartbeat rang out in the room. "We found out with our first, as is tradition on Palaío, though I was pregnant before we got married, which was a new tradition for Palaío!"

Eleni let out a giggle as she looked at Calla. "Those photographers followed me for months, guessing that I'd conceived before the wedding, though we've never officially confirmed it."

"It's none of their business." Calla nodded as she grabbed the gel. "This will be cold." She looked at Kostas. "We should get warmers for the gel. It isn't cold for long, but warm gel is better." Then she turned her attention back to Eleni, ignoring him completely. "So you and Ioannis are going for surprise on the sex for this little one. How fun."

He noticed Calla didn't have any issue using his brother's first name. That shouldn't hurt. He bit his lip as he looked at Calla, wishing they were someplace else. Anywhere else.

Eleni sighed as the wand found the heartbeat. "We are. I put my foot down and demanded we do something different. Traditions are nice, but change can be good too."

His sister-in-law didn't look at him, but Kostas knew the message was intended for him. She had never cared about traditions. Raised in a neighboring kingdom by a royal mother and commoner father, Eleni was the breath of fresh air the monarchy needed.

She and Ioannis had fallen for each other hard and quickly. Their love was evident to anyone paying the smallest bit of attention. Still, the press had had a field day with her. Insinuating that she wasn't royal enough for the king of Palaío, wasn't queen material, wasn't virginal—which wasn't a requirement, or their business, to use Calla's words.

It was only because of her parents—who had refused to cower under the press's long eye and had instilled that in their daughter—that Eleni had not only survived but thrived in the environment. As she'd demonstrated today, she loved messing with the press. Sending them on wild-goose chases. In her words, if they were dumb enough to chase her outlandish statements after she'd established that she liked to tell them nonsense, that was their problem.

His brother had found his match. Kostas was happy for him, but most women hadn't grown up in the "I don't care what anyone thinks" environment that Eleni had.

"Don't you have a patient to prep for?" Calla's tone wasn't hostile, but she'd dismissed him. There was no need for him to hover. No professional need anyway.

"How have you felt this week? Any contractions, cramps? Discomfort?" Calla didn't look at him as he stepped toward the door.

"Discomfort? Have you met any almost-nine-months-pregnant women who are comfortable? I'd love to meet such a mythical creature…and destroy her!"

Calla's laugh joined Eleni's, and Kostas's heart clenched. The two women could be friends… sisters.

No. He pushed the selfish thought away. They'd had a perfect night. That had to be enough.

CHAPTER FOUR

"HAVE A GOOD NIGHT, Calla. Don't stay much longer!" Alexa called as she waved and headed for the clinic door.

Calla waved back and walked into the break room to gather her lunch bag and purse. The clinic was nearly silent—a weird sensation. The clinics and hospitals she'd worked all had quiet periods, but they were never silent.

She, Alexa and the other midwife lived close enough to the clinic that unless a mother had recently given birth, they didn't maintain a twenty-four-hour presence. Even Kostas's palace was less than fifteen minutes from the clinic. A commute that most doctors in Seattle would love.

In the unlikely event that all of them were unavailable, Dr. Stefanios had agreed to be on call for Kostas. It was a tiny clinic, despite its location in Palaío's capital city, and yet Kostas had avoided her for the last week and a half. Except for her first day when she'd treated Queen Eleni, he was always with a patient or in the office, with the door closed, when she was free.

In a larger facility with a staff twenty times larger than the ten on rotation here, it might happen. In Seattle, she'd had friends who shifted from night to day shift, and she occasionally wouldn't see them for a few weeks. But in a clinic this size, it had to be intentional, and she was tired of it. She crossed her arms and looked at the closed office door. Calla felt her brows knit together as she stared at the door.

She could barge in, but a better idea crossed her mind. Calla wasn't waiting for Prince Kostas to simply acknowledge her presence anymore. She was not leaving the island before her contract was up. Besides, she liked it here.

It felt like her place; a weird sensation for a woman who'd never left Seattle before traveling halfway around the world. Her apartment was nice and walking on the warm beach every morning had done more for her soul than she'd thought possible.

Her contract was a year, with the opportunity to extend, if there was a need. She and Kostas didn't have to be friends. Calla doubted that was truly possible after the night they'd shared, but she refused to be ignored.

Dropping her lunch bag on the receptionist's desk, Calla sauntered over to the main door, opened it and then closed it. She knew the buzzer in the office would register the movement, and Alexa's goodbye had been loud enough to hear in every corner of the facility. Kostas knew she was the last midwife in the clinic—and that it was past the end of her shift.

"Ten…nine…eight…" She leaned against the door as she started her countdown. Kostas opened the office door, and she let out a frustrated sigh. "Didn't even let me get to five."

An emotion blipped across his eyes before the mask he'd worn the first morning resettled. "Five?"

"I opened the door—" Calla pushed away from her perch, trying to keep the bubble of emotions roaming through her body in check "—then started counting backward from ten." It was childish, but at least it should silence the final tiny bead of hope that she'd misread the situation. That he'd just been really busy.

Better to accept the truth than give in to any wishful thinking. "You don't have to worry that I think there is more to our night together. Or that I will ruin your reputation, Your Highness." She offered a low bow before reaching for her lunch bag.

"It's not my reputation that's the problem, Calla."

Her name on his lips stilled her feet. But it was his words that lit a fire in her belly. Liam had said it was her upbringing, her lack of societal connections, and her below-average bank account that had riled his parents. Not that her ex had argued with them.

And he'd only been a rich jerk.

Maybe she wasn't the right girlfriend for a prince, but that didn't mean he was any better than her. "*My* reputation is just fine, Your Highness. Maybe it's not good enough for you." Angry tears coated her eyes, but she refused to let them fall. "However, I will not be told that I am less than someone else again."

"Again?" Kostas's head popped back as he took another step toward her.

Calla straightened her shoulders. "You're not the first man to tell me I'm not enough. However, we are colleagues and you should act like it. Treat me just like any of the other midwives." A single tear fell and she wiped at it, furious that she'd lost control. She needed to get out of there; confronting him was a bad idea.

"I can't do that, Calla."

His hand gripped her wrist and she hated the heat climbing up her body, hated that she wanted him to hold her even as he dropped his grip. Why couldn't her body accept what her brain had? Prince Kostas didn't want her.

Men hadn't wanted her before. It had stung then, but it ached with Kostas.

"I'm not saying you aren't enough." He dragged a hand through his hair then shook his head. "You aren't like the other midwives. I've never..." He stepped even closer to her, the distance between them shrinking to millimeters.

When he didn't finish his sentence, she raised an eyebrow and finished it for him. "You never slept with them? Never told them goodbye at an airport, expecting you'd never have to see them again? Never pretended not to know them when fate threw you back together?" The words flew from her lips as she glared at him. Finally, giving in to the hurt and fury his inattention caused.

She'd put herself through nursing school. Come around the world to work on an island where she knew no one. Calla Lewis was perfect the way she was.

"I see I'm interrupting." Eleni's voice carried over the room.

Calla blinked as she stepped back from Kostas. The queen looked from Calla to Kostas, her dark eyes holding her brother-in-law's for far longer than was comfortable. "I apologize. Evan, my bodyguard," she added looking at Calla, "recommended using the rear entrance. I was on my way back from an engagement and wanted to see if you were coming to dinner tonight, Kostas. I didn't want the press to worry about the baby, but..." She shrugged. "I'll see myself out."

Calla raised her chin, knowing she looked tiny compared to Kostas and Eleni. She mustered the last of her reserves as she met the queen's gaze.

"I'm sorry that you had to hear that. I'd appreciate your discretion, Eleni."

"You call her by her first name, but me you refuse to use mine?"

It was a ridiculous complaint, and she chuckled as she grabbed her things. A sad laugh that was the only thing keeping the sobs echoing from her soul. "She acknowledges my presence. I had to trick you to even see you. So, why should I use your name, Your Highness?"

She didn't wait for a response. Just spun on her feet and walked out of the clinic.

"Don't say a word." Kostas turned on his heels without looking at his sister-in-law's face. He'd spent more than a week avoiding Calla. Days of arriving early, staying late, bouncing from one exam room to the next while making sure that she was busy with her patients. It had been torture.

But he couldn't stop his response to her. Even when she was furious with him, all he'd wanted was to beg her forgiveness then spend the rest of the time kissing her. It wouldn't take long for people to notice how he responded to her.

And by trying to protect her from the rapid rumors this island liked to start, he'd made her feel unworthy of his presence. There wasn't enough punishment in the world for that...though he suspected the universe was meting out divine justice by ensuring Eleni had heard everything.

"If you think I have any intention of keeping my mouth shut, then you don't know me at all." Eleni bounced further into the room—well, bounced as much as her heavily pregnant body would allow. "At least now I can tell Ioannis why you have been such a bear. I stopped by unannounced today because I doubted you'd answer your phone."

He wouldn't have, but Kostas left that unsaid.

He'd attended his brother's formal Sunday dinner, which was more meeting than dinner. But he'd taken all his other meals in his private rooms...while thinking of Calla. "I have no intention of discussing this with Ioannis."

Eleni fell into the chair across from the desk and smiled. "I said I would tell Ioannis. I don't care what you do."

He clicked his tongue. "I don't believe that for one moment, Eleni. You absolutely care."

"I do." She grinned. "Your brother knows returning to the island didn't thrill you. He hasn't realized you're plotting your escape yet—"

Kostas opened his mouth but Eleni raised her hand.

"Don't interrupt the queen."

"You only ever pull that card when you don't want to be interrupted."

Eleni continued as though she hadn't heard his mutterings. "Ioannis is busy, but I know what escape looks like. I wore it once myself before I found my place."

"I have a place in Seattle." He forced the words through his teeth. "This island holds nothing for me."

"Calla—"

"Would end up just like Mom or Maria. Devoured by the press and hating me." Heat filled his cheeks as the truth escaped into the room.

Eleni held his gaze for a moment before pushing her body out of the seat. "You are Prince Kostas of Palaío. You can't change that."

She headed for the door. "And Maria was a teenage girl. The rumors your father allowed to circulate were not okay. Do you really think that Ioannis would follow the same path as your father did?"

Kostas wanted to say no. Wanted to think that Ioannis would put his partner before the needs of the crown. But if the pressure was too much... too distracting... He wasn't sure the answer was yes. So he kept his thoughts to himself.

"Your mother..." Eleni paused, weighing her words. "Your father should have protected her. But this generation will not allow someone to get hurt. Especially for this outdated honor code of royals that we 'don't comment to the press.' I comment all the time—exactly as I please."

"Because no one can ever get you to follow the protocol rules."

She waved a hand at him. "I follow the rules, just in my own way. And whoever you fall for will make their own rules, too, if you give them a chance."

He opened his mouth to argue but Eleni had gone without a goodbye. His brother's wife really had a way of making an entrance and delivering her exit.

"Kostas!" Calla's voice echoed from the front of the clinic, and his heart picked up. Finally, she'd called him by his name again. Not Dr. Drakos. Not Your Highness. Kostas.

His joy was short-lived when he saw her holding up a barely lucid Narella.

"Her husband called me," Calla stated as Kostas put his arm on the other side of Narella. "Said she told him she was going to the clinic, but her voice sounded off. Then he couldn't get hold of her. He's on his way now."

Calla shifted, adjusting her position to account for Kostas's height on the other side of the woman. "I found her at the edge of the parking lot, looking confused."

"Feel funny...dizzy...mind foggy." Narella glared at Kostas. "Why are you holding me?"

"She's irritable," Calla whispered and didn't flinch when Narella glared at her. "Any chance of GDM?"

Gestational Diabetes Mellitus, frequently called gestational diabetes, was the most common metabolic disease in pregnancy. He hadn't seen Narella yet, but the symptoms she'd described, combined with the usually warm and bubbly woman's irritability, were classic symptoms.

"Can you tell me how far along you are?" Kostas kept his voice low and comforting as they eased Narella into the exam chair. The woman's pregnancy was showing, but Kostas knew she had at least one child already, and women showed quicker with subsequent pregnancies. Besides, visual pregnancy clues were notoriously unreliable!

"Twenty…" she panted as she looked at him, her eyes narrowing in focus as she bit her lip. She knew how far along she was. If she couldn't remember, that was a bad sign. "Twenty something…"

Calla moved to the computer and began pulling up records. "She's twenty-three weeks along. Scheduled for her diabetes test next week. She had GDM with her first and second pregnancies. Probably why she was already walking to the clinic when the symptoms started." Calla moved without him asking to grab the finger test kit from the cabinet.

She handed it to him, and he took it, meeting her gaze. "I suspect this is coming back with a very low blood sugar result. While I do the stick, can you please get a juice box from the fridge?"

They kept several food items for their patients for such situations in the common area and Calla left quickly. "All right, Narella, you're going to feel a prick and then I am going to get a little blood to test."

She nodded, but Kostas wasn't sure how much she'd actually understood of what he'd said. If they were right, they needed to get Narella's blood sugar up quickly.

"Ouch."

"That was the only pinch," Kostas promised as he pulled a little blood into the tester. It dinged just as Calla walked back through the door with two apple juice boxes.

"Forty-two," Kostas stated as Calla put the straw in the juice box and handed it to Narella. It was a good thing she'd thought to bring the second box. Each one only had half a cup of juice, enough to get a woman with low blood sugar— anything below seventy milligrams per deciliter—into the normal range. Below fifty-four was considered a medical emergency. Below twenty, a person could lose consciousness or have a seizure.

Narella drank the juice and, within three minutes, was already acting more like herself. "I'm so sorry. I got a little dizzy and cut up an apple while waiting for my mother-in-law to arrive to watch my two little boys. I can't remember if I ate it…" Her cheeks colored. "My youngest started crying and… I must have forgotten."

"It's easy for that to happen." Kostas kept his tone calm. "I don't know why Dr. Stefanios was waiting to test you for diabetes, but with your previous history, I would have asked you to start testing your blood at week fifteen. Unfortunately, with your history, you will probably have gestational diabetes with each pregnancy. But that doesn't mean you won't have healthy babies."

"It's just…with Marcus and Atticus at home, it's hard to remember to eat at regular intervals." Narella bit her lip as she looked at her fingers. "I'm not complaining. I love them, but it's so easy to get distracted, and Atticus is still in diapers."

Calla slid onto the corner of the exam chair and patted Narella's knee, waiting for the woman to meet her gaze before she said, "I bet you are a super mom. Two boys under the age of five and pregnant with your first daughter…you *are* amazing. Being tired and distracted is normal, but the best thing you can do for the boys and your daughter is to take care of yourself."

"Easier said than done."

"It is," Kostas agreed. Expectant mothers had so much to deal with, and he wanted to make sure Narella knew he understood that. "But taking care of yourself is the best thing you can do for your children. A healthy mom, a happy mom, a well-rested mom—those are the best things you can give your children."

"Dr. Drakos is right." Calla grinned as she picked up the finger stick test. "It's been about fifteen minutes. Want us to stick you or want to do it yourself?"

Narella glared at the small device before she held out her hand. "I may as well get used to doing it again." She pricked her finger and sighed as the monitor registered sixty-five. "So close." She held out her other hand. "Guess it's another juice box for me."

"Two or three sips should get you to seventy, if you don't want to drink the whole thing," Calla encouraged as she stood.

"Narella! Narella!" Carlos, Narella's husband, raced into the room. "Are you all right, my love?"

His wife waved a hand and gestured to the blood testing kit in her lap. "I have gestational diabetes. Again." Her bottom lip shook as the first tear rolled down her cheek.

Carlos slid next to his wife and pulled her into his arms. "I'm sorry."

"Why don't we give you a few minutes?" Kostas nodded to Calla.

"I'll test my sugar again in fifteen minutes." Narella hiccupped as the sobs racked her body. Carlos kissed the top of his wife's head.

Kostas and Calla quietly stepped from the room.

"Will you want to keep her overnight, Dr. Drakos? I am the midwife on call tonight." The energy that allowed them to work so seamlessly together evaporated as the door to their patient's room closed.

"Calla…"

"Just answer the question, please, Doctor. I don't want to discuss anything else."

Her bottom lip shook, and Kostas wished for the thousandth time since he'd met her that he was simply Dr. Drakos.

"If this was her first experience with GDM, I would. But she and her husband know the symptoms and are skilled at managing the disease."

"Do you need anything else from me tonight?"

"Yes." The word was out before Kostas could think through the moment. But he didn't wait to consider backtracking. "I need to check back in on Narella and her husband. Let them know they can go home, assuming her blood sugar came into the normal range with that second juice box. Can you wait in the office? Or out here…just wait. Please."

Calla crossed her arms, but she didn't argue or head into the office.

That was fine. He owed her an apology. And the knowledge that it wasn't her reputation that was the problem…at least not in the way she assumed.

* * *

Calla waited until Kostas headed back to the patient's room before heading to the small break room. Maybe it was petty. She knew he wanted to discuss her outburst, and she didn't want to do that in the waiting room. But the office was his space.

The midwives used it, but rarely. That was the realm of Dr. Drakos and whomever was hired to join him. Having a personal discussion in his space wasn't what she wanted.

Calla tapped the edge of the wall with her toe and wished she had the strength to just walk away. There was part of her that wanted— needed—an explanation. But if Kostas expected her to apologize for this evening, he was going to be waiting a long time.

She heard Narella and her husband offering their thanks to Kostas and her stomach tightened. Any moment Kostas would find her and say…whatever she hadn't allowed in her pique this evening.

Calla hated to admit that she'd been proud that she'd left without listening to him. It was something she'd never gotten to do with Liam. He'd always had the last statement in any disagreement.

But it hadn't brought her as much satisfaction as she'd hoped.

Because Kostas isn't Liam!

Why couldn't her brain stop that thought?

She'd known the man for less than twenty-four hours and had spent the night with him. That didn't mean she knew him.

He'd had plenty of time during their time together to mention he was a prince. And he hadn't. Hadn't said where he was going or shared anything too personal.

Their connection was physical. Primal, even... but that was all.

So why was her heart so certain that Kostas was somehow different?

Before she contemplated that meandering nonsense, Kostas walked in. His tall frame filled the doorway, and she waited for him to step closer, but he kept his distance. That should make her happy...but rational thought was not something she excelled at in his presence.

When he didn't say anything, she shrugged. "I guess you didn't need anything, Dr. Drakos."

"I owe you an apology."

"Just one?" Calla flinched at her tone and closed her eyes as she rocked back on her heels. "That was uncalled for."

"No." Kostas's voice was warm as it filled the room. "It was very called for. I owe you so many apologies. I should have told you who I was in Dayton."

He pushed a hand through his hair and a muscle in his cheek twitched.

Was the nervous tic not as satisfying with his now short hair?

"Dr. Drakos, OBGYN, is the title that I love. The one that I wish defined me. It's the one I earned. When I'm not here, I try to forget that I have a hereditary title. I'm second in line to the throne, soon to be third. I will never be king, and I am fine with that. More than fine."

He shook his head as he looked at her, his eyes studying her. "When you met me, I was Dr. Kostas Drakos. Still am. Unfortunately, Prince Kostas is the only one that matters on this island."

"That's not true." The denial shot from her lips. This was not the conversation she'd meant to have. Not the one they should have. But the words kept coming, "The people here refer to you by Dr. Drakos or Kostas more than they call you 'Prince' or 'Your Highness.' You are more than your title. If you want to be."

She hated the look in his eyes. She'd seen it reflected in her mirror so often. The look of unworthiness. She'd done her best to banish it from her own gaze, following her relationship with Liam, but she knew how insidious the element was. How it lied to you; convinced you it was true even when all the evidence everyone else saw was crystal-clear.

She didn't know why Kostas, a doctor and a prince, felt unworthy. But he did.

"Maybe."

There was the word that really meant no, but she would not press him. Only he could find his worthiness within the life he had.

"Doesn't change the fact that I reacted badly when I saw you in the clinic the first day. I'd spent my three days on the island imagining you, trying to figure out if there was a way to contact you when..." His voice faltered and he shook himself.

"Then you were here, and Alexa was watching, and the press was outside. It kept me from doing what I actually wanted, or even treating you like a colleague that I'd watched work through a medical emergency in the most amazing way I'd ever seen.

"I am truly sorry, Calla. And I am sorry that after fumbling everything so badly, I avoided you. It was unprofessional."

Those were a lot of words. A lot to work through. "What's wrong with my reputation?"

It wasn't the only question hovering in her mind, but it was the one she needed an answer to. Maybe hearing him say out loud that an American nurse, a broke American nurse, wasn't the ideal candidate for a royal girlfriend would stop the fantasy invading her nightly dreams.

"Nothing is wrong with your reputation."

"You said—"

"I know what I said and how you interpreted it, Calla."

Kostas took a step toward her and Calla desperately wanted to close the distance. But she forced her feet to remain still. She pulled her arms even tighter around herself as she waited for him to continue.

"Calla." Her name slipped from his lips and her skin ignited.

What was the hold he had over her?

"You are perfect. It's me that's the problem." He continued before she could respond. "I know what happily ever after with a secret prince looks like in the movies. I've seen the holiday specials that people binge where everything falls into place with the royal and the baker or journalist or…"

"Nurse?" Calla added as his dark eyes held hers.

"Or nurse." Kostas nodded. "Multiple photographers have captured my picture every day since I returned to this island. There are rumors about my advancing age—"

"Advancing age!" Calla let out a laugh then wished she could pull it back in when the lines on his forehead deepened. "Kostas, you're what? Thirty-seven?"

"Thirty-eight." He grinned at her and took another step forward. "Anyone attached to me, even in a rumor, will be hounded by the island press. It is brutal for those caught in the trap."

That wasn't a guess. She heard it in his voice.

He'd watched others ensnared and hurt. He'd been protecting her. It was sweet in a messed-up, internal trauma way.

"Someone you loved was caught in it?" It was a personal question, and one she wasn't sure he'd answer. But she saw the pain hovering in his eyes.

"Loved is a strong word, though I guess all first relationships feel like love, particularly as a teen. My girlfriend, Maria...the press hounded her. It was stressful but she laughed about it. Until a supposed friend of hers told the press that she'd gotten pregnant and lost the baby."

"Oh..." Calla covered her mouth at the horror of that rumor.

"She left the island not long after. She's happily married now, but on the few occasions she returned to visit her parents, she'd always been greeted by at least one or two journalists. I heard a few years ago that she pays for her parents to visit her now. She doesn't come home because of me."

"That's terrible." It was, but it also wasn't his fault. He hadn't spread the rumor...

"It is." Kostas agreed before Calla could think of anything else to say. "I still should have talked to you. Should have explained." He pulled at the back of his neck as he looked at her. "Can we start over...as professionals? Colleagues?"

"Colleagues." She nodded, hoping the hurt

in her heart wasn't radiating through her voice. "We work well together. We've proved that twice now." She winked, hating the feelings crawling through her.

She wanted to scream at him. To tell him that what was between them might be special. Maybe it was really something. Couldn't they at least try?

But perhaps he was right. Maybe all the emotions, the voice in the back of her head pleading that what they'd shared was special, was just fantasy breaking through.

He was right; life wasn't made for television movies. Even when you really wanted it to be. It was time for her to leave before all her rambling thoughts slipped past her lips. No sense embarrassing herself when they'd finally addressed the issues between them.

"Good night, Kostas." She slipped past him, so close that a bit of his heat touched her shoulder. *No, that's more fantasy, Calla.*

"Good night, Calla."

CHAPTER FIVE

"YOU MADE A FACE!"

Laughs erupted from the break room where the midwives were all enjoying their lunch. Kostas grabbed his lunch and started for his office. This was one aspect of being back in Palaío that Kostas didn't mind.

In Seattle, he saw patients from the time the practice opened until it closed and then did hospital rounds. His meals were usually snacks from vending machines and sad little sandwiches that he'd picked up from the hospital cafeteria. This clinic took an hour and a half lunch break every day. The nurses on staff always gathered in the break room.

He hesitated at the door to his office. It was lonely, and his feet ached to turn. He looked at the break room. He'd kept to himself, but what if today he joined them?

Assuming they didn't mind.

He stepped to the door and all the heads turned toward him. But it was Calla's eyes that he sought. The hazel eyes that haunted his dreams met him with a smile as he raised his lunch bag. "Mind if I join you all?"

"We'll be angry if you don't, now that you're here." Alexa winked at Calla and Kali. "Besides, maybe you can answer the question of what is wrong with our ketchup."

"There's nothing wrong with it." Calla blew out a heavy breath as Kali and Alexa laughed. "It's good. It's just not..."

"Not right." Kali nodded as Calla's cheeks heated. "I worked all night making this recipe. It's my great-grandmother's."

"Kali—you and I both know that your husband is the cook in your family." Alexa nudged Calla before passing the dish of ketchup and the cut-up homemade fries to Kostas.

"You've been in the States for so long. Tell us, Dr. Kostas, what is wrong?"

He dipped the fry while holding Calla's gaze. The tomato paste was delicious. He let out a small sigh as he reached for another fry.

"Well, he likes it. You can leave the island, but you can't really go."

He mentally flinched at that statement, or maybe it wasn't just a mental flinch, since Calla was looking at him with concern. Reaching for a third fry, Kostas dipped the fry and brought it to his lips. "It's delicious, but it's not sweet."

"Sweet?" The other midwives both put hands

over their hearts as they looked from Calla to Kostas.

Calla nodded. "Yes. It's not sweet like the ketchup I grew up with. I mean, it's good, just not ketchup."

"It's Greek ketchup." Kali shook her head. "Better."

Calla laughed, dipped a fry in the ketchup, though Kostas noticed it wasn't the full dip he'd seen her use at the restaurant. "The fries are the best."

"Pish!" Kali waved a hand. "Tomorrow, I'm trying again. We'll find something you like."

"That's sweet, but unnecessary." Calla reached for Kali's hands and squeezed them tightly.

The jealousy and need flipping through him surprised Kostas. The midwives were close. Friends… But he didn't think he could be friends with Calla. Not really. Not when it wasn't what he craved. Tomorrow he'd eat in his office, but it was too late to retreat now.

"Guess I should have put a few bottles in my luggage." Calla giggled. "Can you imagine at the airport? 'Ma'am, is there anything fragile in your bag?' 'Yes, sixteen bottles of ketchup.'"

Her laughter filled the room. It was such a delicious sound. One he loved hearing. "You know a plastic bottle wouldn't break."

"But the ketchup in glass bottles is so much better."

Kostas chuckled and leaned forward. "So it isn't just the sugar-filled tomato paste, but also the type of container?"

"Sure." Calla grinned. "If one is going to be a connoisseur, one must have tried all brands and delivery mechanisms. The best is the pumps at fast-food chains." She brought the tips of her fingers to her lips and kissed them.

The motion was silly, fun, and just so Calla, it made Kostas's heart shudder.

"A connoisseur of ketchup." Kostas shook his head as he reached his hand out to Calla. "That is the most ridiculous thing—" He made eye contact with Alexa. Her mouth was hanging open; he cut his gaze to Kali and saw the same look of astonishment hovering in her eyes.

Kostas swallowed as he leaned back in his chair, adding inches of space between him and Calla, when all he wanted was to lean closer. He'd nearly grabbed her hand in front of the other midwives. And they'd both noticed.

How could they not?

"I know it's ridiculous." Calla's voice was less cheerful now, and that killed him, too.

"But…" She brightened as she looked at Kali and Alexa. "We all have our silly things. Mine is ketchup."

"Kali's is snow globes!" Alexa laughed. "She has dozens of them on their own bookshelves."

"I love when the glitter and pretend snow falls

over the little cityscapes. But you collect haunted dolls, Alexa!"

"That was a secret! And they are not haunted—"

"Just ugly," Kali countered.

The room erupted in giggles as Alexa happily slapped the table. "It started with one sad-looking doll that my youngest just loved. When she outgrew it, I couldn't get rid of her. Now...well, now it's a bit over the top." She shrugged, "But I just see the dolls previously loved by some little girl or boy and then left."

"You are such a bleeding heart." Kali winked at the midwife and Kostas thought the women had forgotten him. Until all three eyes met his.

"What?"

"Oh, come on, Dr. Kostas." Calla's voice was light, teasing, as her eyes held his. "We all shared what our weird thing was, now you."

"I don't have a weird thing." Kostas took another bite of his lunch as he met each of the ladies' eyes equally. He hoped Alexa and Kali would ignore the attention he'd given Calla earlier if he focused on everyone now.

"You do." She grinned as the other midwives nodded.

"Calla is right." Alexa nodded. "Everyone has the thing that makes them happy, that most people look at a little awkwardly. A movie you watch on repeat that's embarrassing. A food. A love of weird snow globes—"

"Or creepy abandoned dolls." Kali countered, and the table shifted.

"Ouch!" Calla's mouth fell open as she playfully glared at Kali. "That hurt."

"Sorry—" Kali looked genuinely upset "—I meant to kick Alexa."

The women laughed again, and he thought for one second that he might have gotten off the hook, but once more all eyes turned to him. He hated to disappoint them. But he couldn't think of a single thing like what they'd discussed.

His room at the palace was luxurious, but he hadn't chosen anything. In fact, no one ever asked his opinion on the décor. Kostas forced the last bite of his lunch into his mouth, swallowed, then offered the truth. "I can't think of a single thing. Being royal means conforming."

Kali giggled. "Conforming. You used to tell the press exactly what you thought of your father. I didn't think the Prodigal Prince knew how to conform."

"It was a hard-learned lesson. But even prodigal princes can learn." He winked at Alexa then looked to Calla.

She held his gaze for a moment, a look he couldn't quite understand on her face. He forced his eyes down; it would be easy to lose himself in their depths…again.

And Alexa and Kali would notice a second misstep.

The chime echoed in the break room, and Alexa and Kali both stood. They quickly exited together, making excuses for why the patient was most likely one of theirs and not Calla's or his. His hope that they might not have noticed the tension between them evaporating on their quickly moving heels.

"You have something." Calla tapped her fingers on the table. Did she yearn to reach across the table, like he did?

"I don't. My room at the palace…"

"What was in your apartment in Seattle?" Calla arched an eyebrow. "Not the palace. But what did you always bring home?"

He wished he had an answer for her. Wished he'd branched out more while in Seattle. His apartment hadn't been a home. It was simply a place he slept. The walls were blank, the cabinets full of white dishes, even the bedspread was a light gray. It held no personality.

"I know you want to hear about the funny mug I bought that said 'A Wise Doctor Once Wrote…' and then it has a bunch of unrecognizable scribbles on it. But I don't have anything like that."

"Oddly specific mug choice." Calla boxed up the containers she'd brought her lunch in and stood. "You wanted that mug, didn't you?"

"It was funny. There was another one next to it that said something far too vulgar for the office, but it made me laugh." He'd picked both up, nearly bought them, then put them back on the shelf.

Before he could say anything, she leaned close. His heart leaped at the light floral scent. The same scent he'd lost his mind to the night he'd made love to her. The urge to kiss her, to throw all his caution away, raced through him.

"Don't worry, I won't tell anyone you like funny coffee mugs—even if royals don't buy said mugs."

Then she was gone.

Calla looked at the closed office door then back at the small box in her hands. She'd found it in a shop that catered to tourists. After looking in far too many shops for the perfect one.

She bit her lip and tried to make herself walk to the door. He wasn't avoiding her…at least not like the first week. Instead, over the last week, he'd reverted to the perfect doctor with no time for small talk or lunch breaks. He'd even scheduled clients during his lunch hour.

She was pretty sure he was surviving on granola bars and yogurt. That, she knew, was common in US practices overextended with patients, but taking a break here was a perk. One she had no intention of giving up unless a mother was in labor.

It was hard not to blame the interaction they'd had over ketchup. Alexa and Kali had each privately asked if something was going between her and Kostas. She'd answered honestly…no.

And it had broken her heart to do so.

There was no reason for her to get him a gift. Particularly one so intimate…

It's a coffee mug, Calla.

But it felt intimate. She knew something about Prince Kostas she was almost certain he'd never shared with anyone else.

Shaking herself, she stepped up to the door. Colleagues could get each other a gift.

Please, Calla.

Justifying wouldn't change the truth. She'd gone looking for a mug for Kostas. She'd examined funny mugs, sweet mugs, silly mugs, even a few not-safe-for-work mugs. Then she'd found the exact one he'd wanted. The shopkeeper had checked on her after she'd squealed in delight.

Running her fingers over her heated cheek, she shifted the box and raised her hand to knock. Before her hand connected, the door opened and Kostas looked down at her. His dark gaze seemed to trip over her, like he wanted to let it linger but didn't dare.

Man, my brain really is going overboard!

"You don't have to knock, Calla. The office is for everyone."

"Yet you're the only one hiding in it." She shrugged, hoping her voice was light. She was teasing…mostly. Calla missed seeing him.

She shouldn't. But knowing that and understanding why she felt so drawn to the man in front of her were two very different things.

"I could argue that I'm busy and not hiding." Kostas winked before stepping back to let her into the office.

"But you'd be lying." Calla winked back as he closed the door.

The air in the office thickened as his eyes held hers. The tension stringing between them felt it might materialize any minute. Though, since Alexa and Kali had asked if they were secretly dating, maybe it was visible to the naked eye.

"I got you something." Kostas's words caught her off guard as he slid around the desk, his hip brushing hers.

"I got you something too." Calla held up the box and laughed as he held out one that was wrapped in fine paper with an enormous bow. It looked like something that belonged on a movie set.

She'd seen pictures in magazines of fancy and, she assumed, empty boxes. Advertisements for gifts she couldn't afford, but no one had ever wrapped something for her in such a fine manner.

She looked from the plain box in her hand to his package and felt heat creep into her cheeks again. Calla hadn't even considered wrapping the mug. The difference between them truly on display with two gifts. "I didn't wrap yours, though. I, um…"

Kostas moved to her side as she held up the plain brown box. His fingers slid over hers as he lifted it from her. Fire coiled in her belly as she fought the urge to lean close. To rise on her tiptoes and drop a light kiss on his lips.

"Ladies first." His deep voice swirled around her as he picked up the beautiful package.

She reached for the box, surprised by its hefty weight. "You didn't wrap a box of rocks, did you?" She carefully peeled the tape from the edge of the corner. It felt almost wrong to destroy the pretty wrapping.

When she finally got the paper off, Kostas let out a sigh. "I wasn't sure you'd ever actually unwrap it."

"It's too pretty!" Calla pushed her hip against his. She regretted the connection immediately as her body burst with need.

Turning her head, she focused on the present. Not sure what he would have thought to get her… and wrap like it was worth a small fortune. Lifting the lid off, she couldn't stop the gasp. "Kostas!" Tears and laughter warred with each other as she tugged the first jar of ketchup from the paper-lined box.

Six jars of ketchup. The real deal.

"No matter how many recipes the other midwives have you try, they won't be the same as these."

"No. Though all the recipes have been good but not the same. Thank you." She pushed the tear away from her cheek as she held the precious condiment. "Sorry, homesickness hasn't really hit me. But I just got a wave of it. Over ketchup!"

Kostas took the bottle from her hands, putting it back in the box before he pulled her into his chest.

She sighed as his heat wrapped around her. The comfort of the hug, one traveler to another. He'd left Palaío, undoubtedly dealt with homesickness even though he'd been happy to be away from the title of prince, then made a life for himself in Seattle. Did he miss the rainy mornings like she did? The gray sky and moss-covered green buildings?

His home country was beautiful, but it was so different.

She inhaled, loving the scent of sea and mint that floated through her. Kostas. She squeezed him tightly then stepped back.

"All right, enough homesickness." *And wantonness!* "It's not as good as a month's worth of ketchup—"

"A month? I assumed that would get you through at least six." He grinned as he opened the plain box she had given him, his mouth falling open as he lifted the mug from the box.

He held it carefully as he spun it from front to back. It had the same design on both sides: "A Wise Doctor Once Wrote…" followed by a bunch of illegible writings.

The silence stretched out as he stared at it.

Had she guessed wrong? Was it a poor gift? Maybe he'd been joking about the mugs. He was a prince, after all.

"It's a pretty popular doctor mug, and you mentioned this one. I found it…" She twisted the toe of her shoe into the floor as embarrassment crawled through her. *Maybe this was dumb.* "I just saw it."

"Calla." Kostas set the mug down and reached for her. His hand ran along her chin as he pressed his lips together. "It's the best gift I've ever gotten."

"I doubt that." Calla trembled as his fingers danced along her skin, the need to kiss him screaming through her.

"I'm not lying or stretching the truth even a little. It's perfect." He looked at her.

There were so many reasons she should pull back. He'd made it painfully clear that he had no interest in seeing her, at least not on the island. He was a prince, heir to an actual crown, and she was the daughter of two hardworking restaurant owners. She had less than a thousand dollars to her name. Cinderella was a fairy tale.

But tonight she wanted a moment to believe the fantasy. A moment to give in. Lifting her head, she brushed her lips against his.

"Calla."

She shuddered as her name fell from his lips. She feared he'd pull away, but he wrapped an arm around her waist, drawing her tightly to him. It felt like coming home, like falling back into the place she was meant to be. It was temporary, but for a few minutes, she was going to cling to the fantasy.

He tasted of mint and the sea, of dreams and everything she couldn't have. It was precious, and it hurt. Calla flung her arms around his neck. Kostas…this was her Kostas.

Not the prince. Just the man she'd connected with weeks ago.

"Calla…"

This time, when her name slipped between them, it was to end the spell capturing them. She didn't cling to him, even though part of her wanted to. Instead, she stepped back, wrapping her arms around herself, hoping to keep some of his heat close to her.

"You don't have to say anything, Kostas. I know this—" she gestured between them "—isn't what you want."

He tilted his head, and she saw the flash of pain in his eyes. "The moment I saw you in this clinic, I wanted to pull you into my arms. Wanted to kiss you. Thank the fates that somehow, despite all the odds, you'd landed on my island."

"But..."

"Royal life isn't easy, Calla. Fairy tales are fantasy."

"Actually, the original fairy tales were allegorical morality lessons. The little mermaid turns to sea foam when she falls in love with the prince she can never have." Calla bit her lip as the explanation bubbled forth.

Kostas reached for her hand, his thumb rubbing along the edge of her palm. "Calla..." He closed his eyes, as if weighing something, then opened them. "If we try this, you'll be hounded. I need you to understand."

Her heart raced as the conversation's turn sprinted through her. "If we try..."

"Maria isn't the only woman I've seen destroyed by this." He sighed as she squeezed his hand, unsure of where the conversation was heading but wanting him to know that she was there.

"My mother... She left. Royal life was too much for her. She..."

He swallowed and Calla could see the pain radiating through him.

"Mom, Queen Sofia, was so beautiful. She did everything my father and the country had asked of her. But it wasn't enough. Her quiet answers, her shy smile, were manipulated into stories of her being stuck up. Of her thinking she was better than the rest of the island's inhabitants."

The words tumbled forth as she stepped closer to him and put her head on his shoulder. Just letting him know she was there while he got everything out.

"My father thought it was beneath the palace to respond. She tried to bear it. We're taught that from the cradle. Duty. Responsibility. Country first. She tried—she did. But…"

"But it was too much?" Calla offered.

"It was. One day she left for vacation and never came home. They never spent another night under the same roof."

He laid his head against hers. "Even leaving didn't bring her peace. She died when I was thirteen. She was swimming in the ocean and…" He sucked in a deep breath.

"She was a strong swimmer, but there were reporters on the beach. I swear she couldn't seem to escape them. In the end, the press trapped her. We think she tried to swim down the shoreline a little and got caught in a riptide. But, honestly, we don't know."

"Oh, Kostas." She pulled him into her arms, gripping him with all her strength. "I'm so sorry."

He took a deep breath and smiled at her. "She

would have loved you." The words seemed to surprise him. His eyes widened and his mouth fell open, but nothing came out. She squeezed him and kissed his cheek.

"It would have been nice to meet her," Calla stated, fully meaning it.

Kostas kissed the top of her head and offered her a smile that didn't fully reach his eyes. "I don't usually speak of Mom, but I want you to understand—really understand— what dating a royal means."

"I see." Calla tried to find the right words. So many emotions were floating through her.

"I wish it wasn't the case. But your life will be controlled by things that rarely make sense— royal protocols, questions, cameras. Your life won't truly be your own. And it doesn't end when we break up, either. You'll always be the nurse that dated the royal."

When we break up...

Those words sent ice through her. *When* not *if.*

She'd been willing to try it. Willing to see if she could make life work within the confines he saw for himself and the person he cared for. The connection between them was something she'd never felt.

Except, Kostas saw this as temporary—which most relationships were—but she wouldn't enter one where one partner already knew there was an expiration date.

"I understand." She swallowed as she looked at the mug on the desk next to the bottles of ketchup. Such silly presents, things that shouldn't matter. But they spoke of the connection between them. The prince and the nurse… Kostas and Calla.

Her heart ached as she grabbed the box of ketchup bottles and hugged it to her tightly. This was the crossroads, and she wanted to walk the other path, the one that ended with her in his arms again. But not if he thought their relationship was already destined for failure.

She didn't trust herself to say anything. Instead she looked at the ketchup and then at him. "Thank you for telling me all of that, Kostas. For trusting me with the memories of your mom." She swallowed the pain and added, "I'll ration these…well, I'll at least try."

"Good night, Calla." His voice was wistful, like he'd hoped she'd have agreed to a fling. Despite the knowledge that he didn't see her as a potential partner for life.

Liam hadn't seen her as a forever partner, either. At least Kostas had said the words up front.

Calla Lewis was worth more than temporary, even if her heart cried out for it.

Kostas had put distance between them and she'd pushed past it. Demanded he acknowledge her. She didn't regret that choice, but now she'd make sure to protect herself.

"Goodbye, Kostas."

"Dr. Drakos?" Alexa slid into the office, her head down.

Kostas lifted the mug Calla had gotten him to his lips as he looked at the normally relaxed and chatty midwife. His coffee had cooled in the last hour, but it was the mug he was reaching for, not the coffee.

Whatever Alexa had to say, he doubted it was good.

It was ridiculous that a mug from a woman who'd done her best to avoid him the last two days brought him comfort, but he didn't question it. Just like he didn't question Calla's putting the distance between them after he'd laid out the truth about what dating him looked like. And when she decided she'd had enough, her life wouldn't go back to normal. At least not while she was on Palaío.

He'd never tire of her. Of that he was nearly certain, though he shouldn't be. He'd known the woman for one spectacular night and worked with her for a little over two months now. It wasn't enough time. But his soul knew it.

If Calla had stepped into his arms the other night, told him she wanted to try it, he'd have kissed her deeply. Given her directions to the private entrance of the palace and spent the night worshipping her. He pushed those feelings aside as he looked at Alexa.

"What's wrong?" He waited briefly then added, "Is it a patient?" He doubted that. Alexa was boisterous and fun, but when a patient was involved, she was all business...and straight to the point.

"I was joking with my neighbor the other day and I said something I shouldn't have." She looked up at him, her eyes filled with unshed tears. "I am really sorry, Your Royal Highness."

The use of his title sent tingles racing across his skin. He kept his voice low and calm as he stood. "I'm sure whatever it was isn't that bad, Alexa."

"They asked how it was working with you, and about the new nurse." Alexa pursed her lips. "You know how tiny the island can feel. Everyone wants to know."

He nodded as tension pulled through his belly. *Calla.* She was an outsider, a beautiful outsider who'd arrived within hours of the Prodigal Prince. "What did you say?"

"That I thought you two would be a cute couple." Alexa's sigh echoed in the small office. "It was a joke. I swear. Gossip about colleagues. I didn't think..."

"Didn't think what?" There was more to the story and Alexa, normally so talkative and bubbly, was dribbling out the information. She pulled her cell from her back pocket, swiped a few times, and put the phone in front of him.

The *Weekly Times*, the main gossip source for the island and its surrounding neighbors, had a picture of Calla leaving the clinic. The photo wasn't overly flattering. There were a million ways they could have gotten a better image…if they'd wanted to.

But the headline made it obvious that the goal of the magazine was not to put Calla Lewis in a good light: Outsider Trying to Infiltrate the Royal Family?

He hated the phrase, but he wasn't sure how Alexa thought this was her fault. "Alexa, this is unfortunate, but, honestly, little has happened since I got back. So making up a story on a slow news day isn't all that surprising." He handed her the phone; he needed to find Calla. Make sure she was okay. But Alexa also needed to know he didn't blame her.

"Remember the story about Ioannis marrying into the British royal family before he wed Eleni? It was complete hogwash. My brother doesn't even know the granddaughter of the British monarch. But the headline got clicks and sold ad space, which is all these rags care about."

"Thank you. I wish I could just accept that." She blew out another breath and scrolled down the page on her phone before putting it back in front of him. "The words from the anonymous source are my words to my neighbor."

Calla and Prince Kostas have a chemistry that is evident to anyone near them. It's like they're drawn to each other. Magnets circling each other, yearning to get close enough to cling together.

"I thought the magnet reference was clever, but now that I see it in print…" Alexa's lip wobbled. "I'll tender my resignation if you'd like."

"That is unnecessary. I wish I was a normal colleague, but I'm not."

"I'm not trying to infiltrate anything! Just delivering babies. Excuse me." Calla's voice carried through from the front of the clinic, and Alexa turned before he could say anything else. He rushed around the desk and was in the waiting room a few seconds after the midwife. But it was already too late. Alexa was explaining and apologizing.

"It's no big deal." Calla hugged the other midwife but kept her gaze away from Kostas, just like she'd done for the last several days.

What he wouldn't do to see those eyes locked on him again…

"Calla, are you okay?"

She laughed. "Of course, Dr. Drakos. I mean, they could have chosen the picture they snapped of me walking on the beach and not the one of me looking spent in my scrubs at the end of a long day."

"The beach? When did that happen?"

"Two days ago." She squeezed Alexa's hand. "I looked good that morning. Already done my hair and makeup. Very put together, which is surprising since I seem to still be battling a touch of jet lag after weeks." She yawned as she shrugged.

Kostas crossed his arms at his chest as the urge to pull her close echoed through him. Someone had taken her photo and she hadn't told him. *Why would she?*

They were colleagues. Not actual magnets. But it hurt that she hadn't mentioned it. Hadn't asked for his aid.

"Are you sure you're okay?" He hated repeating the question. She looked exhausted. And it couldn't be jet lag. Not after almost six weeks on the island. They'd had a night delivery last week, but otherwise, the tempo at the clinic had been fairly light.

Was something else going on? Was there more than just reporters at the beach? Surely they hadn't camped out at her place for one thread of gossip.

Finally, her gaze locked on his. "I'm sure it will all blow over soon, Dr. Drakos. No need to worry about me."

Dr. Drakos. For a few beautiful days, he'd

been Kostas again. But since she'd given him the mug and walked away, she'd reverted to Dr. Drakos again. He hated it.

"If it doesn't…"

"It will." Calla nodded, dismissing any further concerns.

The door to the clinic opened before Kostas could argue. "Calla, I don't feel all that well. Can you please give me a quick exam?"

Eleni's voice pitched higher as she closed the door and then winked at Kostas.

"I do hope Ioannis understands you are just playing the press." Kostas fisted his hands at his sides as his sister-in-law darted to Calla's side.

She'd become Eleni's favorite midwife. Assuming there were no complications with her pregnancy that required him to perform a C-section, it would be Calla delivering the soon-to-be second in line to the throne. The two women got on well, but he hoped Eleni wasn't expecting more.

She knew far more than Alexa had even guessed at. Though he knew she'd tell no one besides Ioannis. The two had no secrets.

He envied them. That had surprised him.

His and Ioannis's parents had had a difficult relationship. Theirs was the last marriage of convenience for the sake of the throne. The throne had come first for his father. No matter what.

Ioannis and Eleni doted on their son. Treated

him as a son rather than as an extension to the throne that bound them all to Palaío.

And they loved each other so very much.

Being near them had sent jealousy crawling through him. But, as Calla's plight currently showed, there were costs associated with falling for a royal. Or having someone assume you had.

"What is going on, Eleni? Or are you just play-acting for the journalists again?" Calla smiled as the queen linked her arm through hers.

Does Calla understand how unique that is? How Eleni is protecting her, in her own way? How she'd protect her if she and Kostas were—

No. He would not travel that worn path.

"Those aren't journalists. They are people hoping to capture a picture or story they can sell. Nothing more." Eleni rubbed her back and cringed. "I went for coffee and figured I'd make an appearance. And my security team can help Kostas's run a bit of interference."

She grimaced. "Wow, my back just aches. Comes and goes in waves, but seriously!" She held up her hand before Kostas or anyone else could comment. "I know how far along I am. I know that at this stage I will be uncomfortable." She sucked in a weighty breath.

"Have you timed the back pain?" Calla asked as she looked at Kostas.

He pursed his lips and looked at the clock as Eleni took a few more deep breaths.

"You think it's labor. I didn't even consider it. It hurts, but it doesn't feel like my labor with Mateo. That one was basically textbook." She looked from Calla to Kostas.

"Back labor is more common when the baby is in an occiput posterior position," Kostas offered.

Eleni glared at him then looked at Calla. "Can you please say that in non-doctor-speak?"

"It means the baby is sunny-side up." Calla's voice was soft and calm. "So the head is pushing against your back instead of facing your stomach. It means nothing to your baby—they'll be fine. However, until they shift, or if they don't, it means labor is going to be tougher for you."

"Oh, great." Eleni scowled and grabbed her back again. "Kostas…" she panted as she forced herself to breathe.

"Get Ioannis?" he asked while she worked through the pain. He'd timed the contractions and at this point they were still about eight minutes apart. Eleni was in labor, but she likely had a way to go yet.

"Yes," she gasped, barely able to keep the bite from her tone. "He put me here."

"Yes, he did," Calla agreed. "Why don't you come with me to the delivery room? I'll rub your back after we get you set up. It will offer a little relief."

"At least the press will have something better

to discuss than Calla infiltrating the royal family now!" Eleni called out as he started for his office.

Calla laughed. "How sweet of you to go into labor for my benefit, Eleni. Not sure it's the tactic I'd have taken, but it makes a statement. How will I ever repay you?"

"If you rub my back, I promise to do anything you want."

Eleni looked up and saw Kostas still standing by the office door, watching the comedy play out. "Ioannis! Now!"

CHAPTER SIX

CALLA YAWNED AND rubbed her back, trying to calm the achy soreness resting there. She knew it was nothing compared to Eleni's intense pain, but after tending to her patients and helping Eleni through her labor, which still hadn't progressed past five centimeters almost twelve hours later, she was exhausted.

The queen had apologized repeatedly for coming to the clinic so early. Eleni had labored at home for most of her first pregnancy, so she honestly hadn't thought the back pain was labor. The jovial woman really had stopped by to joke with Kostas, add a distraction for the gathered horde out front, and let her bodyguards help with crowd management.

It was sweet. But once Ioannis arrived, the small group of hopeful "journalists" that hung around the clinic almost constantly was replaced by the real deal. More crews had arrived throughout the day.

As had palace security.

The clinic was now basically on lockdown until the prince or princess made their arrival.

Any patient who didn't need to be seen today had been rescheduled. That left a handful of women with advanced pregnancies to navigate the crowd. Calla and the other midwives had escorted them through the parking lot, ignoring all the called questions. It was madness!

They'd discussed sending Eleni home a few hours ago. And they'd kept her here rather than ignite more rounds of speculation and questions. Besides, they figured she'd be back in a few hours anyway, which would only restart the whole process. No one had expected a twelve-hour labor...and counting.

"If you're tired, you can go home." Kostas's voice was soft as he stepped into the small break room. "I gave Eleni some Stadol. She's napping now. When she wakes, it will be time to start Pitocin if she hasn't progressed. But hopefully the rest will kick-start things."

Calla hoped the rest worked. She'd seen exhausted mothers who got pain meds, and could finally sleep for a few hours, progress immediately upon waking. Pitocin would ensure the delivery advanced, but it also intensified the contractions.

Eleni's water had broken an hour ago, officially starting the delivery timer. While some research indicated it was safe to labor for at least forty-eight hours following water breaking, many doctors only waited twenty-four hours if the patient was already at the hospital or clinic.

"Calla, if you need rest…"

"I'm fine. I took a nap after my last patient. The bunk beds in the back room are more comfortable than the ones at the birthing center I worked at. I swear they made them from concrete and covered them with foam so they could claim they were beds," Calla joked as she leaned against the wall.

Hopefully, the light tone and humor would cover the exhaustion still coursing through her. She also should have responded to Kostas quicker, but her brain seemed a little foggy these days. Chalk that up to another thing she couldn't quite place.

She wanted to believe she was fine, but if she was honest, it wasn't exactly true. She was tired. Still functional, but her body never seemed to reach fully rested these days. It was like her internal charge could only reach eighty percent. And she couldn't understand why.

She usually fell into her bed and slept straight through the night. If she woke during the night, she had no memory of it.

Today marked eight weeks since her arrival on the island. Long enough by weeks for jet lag to pass. She didn't have a cold or a virus. Calla checked her temperature every morning, just to be sure. She wasn't risking the health of her moms and their newest arrivals.

Maybe it was finally decompressing from years of hectic schedules? The clinic in Palaío was lovely and so much more relaxed than the environment she'd had in Seattle. She routinely saw between seven and ten patients a day here, rather than twenty to twenty-five.

Her delivery schedule was a fourth of what had been in the US. It was the type of nursing she'd longed to practice when she went into the field. She'd be living her best work life, if she wasn't constantly fighting off yawns!

"Do you need anything?"

Kostas's question was quiet, and he wasn't talking about being tired or Eleni.

The urge to lean into him, to tell him she wanted more, was nearly overwhelming. But before she could think of anything, Ioannis stepped into the room, shattering whatever moment they might have.

"Dinner!" Ioannis grinned, the smell of burgers and fries arriving with him. "If either of you tell my wife I snuck a burger while she slept, I will exile you from the island!"

Kostas laughed as he sat in the chair across from his brother. The two looked so alike, but Kostas carried himself differently. A little apart. Like he wasn't fully comfortable.

Because he isn't.

The thought wrapped through Calla's mind as she looked at Kostas. He was the best OBGYN she'd ever worked with. Caring, but firm when necessary. He listened to the midwives, taking their concerns seriously. He was comfortable in the medical world.

It was his title that hung heavy. That, given what he'd told her about Maria and his mother, wasn't surprising. But he couldn't separate the parts of his life, not really. He was both an OBGYN and a prince. If only he could accept that…

She pushed herself off the wall. Tiredness was making her brain wander.

"Not sure your brother considers exile quite the threat." Calla gave Kostas a wink and immediately regretted the decision as his eyes held hers. She'd done so well keeping her distance lately. Not because she wanted to, but it was necessary, and the fluttering in her heart reminded her how easy it was for her to react to the man.

"True." Ioannis playfully pointed at her. "But I could threaten to exile you. That might be enough of a threat."

It took all her control not to lift her hands to her heated cheeks as she watched Kostas for his reaction. Reaching for the burgers and fries, Calla's mouth watered and her stomach rumbled with a hunger she hadn't noticed. It was a thoughtful meal. One she figured Ioannis had requested because she was helping his wife.

"She's one of the best midwives I've ever worked with. No. The best!" Kostas's eyes hovered on her for an instant before turning to his brother. "You don't want to deprive the island of her expertise." His words were the right ones. The ones to diffuse the tension flickering between them.

That didn't mean his rational explanation didn't cut it.

Swallowing, she picked up a fry, enjoying the salty smell. It was just what she wanted. In the last week, she'd craved salty things…another change from her normal sweet tooth. Maybe the island really was turning her into a different person.

"Wait. I brought ketchup!" Ioannis chuckled, clearly trying to smooth over the friction he'd created. If she'd ever doubted whether Eleni had told her husband about the conversation she'd overheard, it vanished.

Ioannis clearly meant to offer the joke, not to cause embarrassment. A brotherly gibe gone too far. He cleared his throat as he pulled the bottle from the bag on the floor. "Kostas spent a small fortune rush shipping the stuff from the States. And I snagged one bottle. I must admit, Calla, that I was pleasantly surprised by the taste. Sweet…"

She looked at the ketchup bottle and forced a smile to her face. The gift from Kostas was one of the kindest things anyone had done for her. But it didn't taste right.

It was tangy…and off. She couldn't quite explain it. She'd opened two bottles, thinking it was something with the first. But the second had tasted strange too.

"What's wrong?" Kostas handed her the ketchup. "And don't say nothing. I can tell."

"How?" Calla raised her chin, daring him to acknowledge he paid more attention to her than he did to anyone else. It was a dumb move. One that could only bring her heartache, but she couldn't retract the question once it was hovering in the air.

"You love ketchup." He waved the bottle at her, waiting for her to take it. "I don't pretend to understand it, but whenever you discuss it or see it, it brings a smile to your face. You frowned just now. So something is wrong."

She bit her lip then ate the fry she was holding, still not reaching for the ketchup. Kostas set the bottle down, his eyebrows knitting as he looked at her.

Her mouth exploded with salt and potato goodness. The fry was delicious, and she reached for another, careful to avoid Kostas's gaze as she answered. "It doesn't taste right."

Calla hated admitting that. She knew how

happy he'd been with the present. It was sweet, but maybe the international transfer…or maybe her tastes on the Mediterranean island were just evolving. Though, she mused, something about her love of burgers and fries had changed.

"I remember when Eleni was pregnant with our first, she suddenly hated clams. She'd loved them before, but never got the taste for them back." Ioannis tossed a fry into his mouth. "I'll admit that I didn't mind when her clambakes went away, and I suspect now that you have found our local fare so much better, you might not want ketchup hiding the taste of such good food!"

She laughed, hoping it sounded right in the quiet room. "Your island's food certainly tastes wonderful. Shame about the clams, though. My parents served a buttery clam dish in their restaurant, but they only served it when there was access to fresh clams. Here, that's never a problem."

A longing for home, for the small kitchen where her parents tried new dishes for their restaurant, threatened to overwhelm her. It was silly. They'd been gone for years. The restaurant long closed. Emotions wrapped around her heart and she had to swallow the sudden swell.

Her feelings seemed closer to the surface. Maybe it was the tiredness or the excitement of a new life waiting to come forth. That had always filled her with wonder before. Something so right about a baby coming into the world, a new life that could travel this world in so many different directions.

"Fresh clams are all over the place on the island. I used to hunt for them for hours on the beach as a boy." Kostas grinned then turned his attention to his brother.

"Shifting topics, I may have found another OBGYN. Remember Dr. Bandi? She's in Greece right now, but looking for a change and a chance to come home."

The men started talking about recruiting another doctor. Any other time, she'd have paid attention to a discussion regarding a new doctor. Nurses and midwives performed a lot of the duties here, but the right, or wrong, physician could seriously impact the clinic. In one of her first positions, the OBGYN's toxic attitude had run off nearly all his nurses within two years.

She should focus on the brothers' conversation, but her ears pounded as she thought through Ioannis's statement about Eleni and clams. Mentally, she calculated back to her last period. Two weeks before she'd arrived in Palaío.

Dear God.

She was late. By several weeks. Calla's throat tightened as she tried to focus on chewing her food and nodding at the right moments.

Kostas chomped on a fry, completely oblivious to the turmoil racing through her.

All her symptoms suddenly made perfect sense. Fatigued, foggy brain, dislike of a once-beloved food…even her breasts were tender. She was a midwife. How had she missed the symptoms in herself that she'd talked about with so many women?

Because she hadn't even considered it a possibility. The only person she'd slept with in the last year was sitting at the table with her. They'd used protection. But how many times had she told stunned women that condoms were only ninety-eight percent effective, even when used perfectly—which she was nearly certain she and Kostas had done.

That meant that out of every one hundred people using that method of contraception, two would get pregnant. She'd seen women thrilled and devastated by such news. But most often it was shock they dealt with first.

She took a bite of her burger, not really tasting it as she tried to force her brain to consider everything. She was pregnant. With Kostas's baby… his royal baby.

"I know you're exhausted, Eleni, but you have to push." Kostas kept his voice level but firm as his sister-in-law glared at him.

"You can do it, honey." Ioannis leaned over to rub his wife's shoulder, and she held up a hand.

"If you touch me, I will hurt you." She let out

a soft sob as she leaned back in the bed. "I'm sorry. I didn't actually mean that. I mean I did but…" Eleni let out a huge sigh as she closed her eyes. "I'm so tired."

"Of course you are," Calla stated. Stepping to the bed, she pulled the pillow off and adjusted the height just a little. "Giving birth is exhausting. There is a reason we call it labor."

Calla pursed her lips as she looked at Kostas. There was a hint of something in her gaze that he couldn't quite place. It was gone before he could consider it…though now wasn't the time.

"I think it's time to try the squat bar." Calla looked at Kostas. "What do you think, Dr. Drakos?"

He nodded. "I agree." She'd been pushing for nearly an hour and hadn't progressed. It was Eleni's second pregnancy; Kostas knew she wanted to avoid a C-section. He glanced at the clock. He'd let her push for another hour, provided she wasn't too exhausted. Then they'd have to do what was best for her and the baby.

The squat bar hadn't been an option at his hospital in Seattle, though he was aware that Calla had experience with them from her work in the birthing center.

"Squat…bar?" Eleni panted.

"Yep." Calla nodded as she helped Eleni to sit back in the bed and then raised the bar from under the bed. "The supine position, or laying on your back, is great for doctors and midwives to monitor your progress. However, some studies indicate it makes delivery for moms more difficult. Delivering in a squat or with a birth chair in the upright position was used for centuries, and still is in many nations. Gravity helping moms!"

She kept her voice bright as she explained the benefits of shifting positions, even for delivery. She was in complete control of the situation, mindful only of her patient's needs. No thought at all that she was directing the queen.

He knew that was one of the reasons Eleni had requested Calla as her primary midwife. When Mateo was born, Dr. Stefanios and the midwives had fluttered around her, paying deference but also not completely sure how to handle the propriety of delivering the queen…no matter how much Eleni had tried to explain that she wanted to be treated just like any other patient.

Calla gave her that. And it was a priceless gift, even if Calla didn't realize it.

"Brace your hands here and then get into a squat. Ioannis, give her a little support and rub her back." Calla guided Eleni, and Kostas let her take the lead while he monitored the baby's vitals.

Just before he'd left Seattle, he'd heard the arguments for birthing upright or even on all fours. The midwives and nurses were pushing for the inclusion of the option, at least. A few of the older OBGYNs had vehemently disagreed, though they'd provided no good reasons.

The nurses had lobbied him, and he'd agreed with them. He'd argued that if it made birthing easier, he'd try anything, as long as it was safe for mom and baby. Unfortunately, Ioannis had summoned him home shortly after. So he hadn't actually delivered a baby in any position besides laying down.

Eleni breathed through her teeth, almost hissing as the next contraction started.

"Brace and push for me." Calla coached as Eleni worked her way through the contraction. "That's it. Push!"

The contraction subsided, but Kostas could see that Eleni was a bit more relaxed, even though she was squatting and leaning against the bar.

"If this is easier, why the lying on your back?"

"A king of France preferred it." Calla laughed as Eleni's mouth fell open.

Kostas knew this story. King Louis the Fourteenth was said to enjoy watching his wives and mistresses deliver babies. Scholars were divided on the reasons, but he noted that Eleni had lost interest as another contraction took over.

"I swear this little girl better appreciate me!" Eleni choked out as she gripped the bar and bore down.

"It's a girl?" Ioannis rubbed his wife's back as

she let out a guttural noise and leaned against the bar as the contraction subsided.

"I dreamed of her last night. Or, at least, I think I did. I dreamed of Mateo just before his birth too." She sucked in a deep breath as she bore down again. "Stubborn too…takes after me."

"It's one of the things I love about you."

"Still want to murder you right now."

Kostas watched Calla bite her lips as she monitored Eleni's progress. She crossed her arms then uncrossed them. Was she worried about something?

The baby's vitals were great, and Eleni was doing fine. Still, Calla seemed off. Her eyes seemed to dart to him then away.

"That's it." Ioannis coached his wife as she bore down and then kissed her forehead when the contraction subsided.

His brother loved Eleni and his son, and soon-to-be daughter—if Eleni was right— more than anything. Kostas's eyes flickered to Calla again, and jealousy flared through him.

He wanted what his brother had. More than he'd ever admitted before meeting Calla. But Ioannis was king. Beloved son of the island.

Ioannis did little wrong, according to the island's inhabitants and the press. Everyone loved Eleni, even though she spoke her mind, because

Ioannis loved her. There was grace given to him that Kostas never received.

Ioannis was perfect. Kostas was the opposite. The foil to his brother. It wasn't true, but truth rarely sold many papers or garnered enough ad clicks to make it worthwhile.

Carefully stated half-truths that skirted libel laws. Particularly when his father had refused to acknowledge any stories about his youngest son. The girl he'd cared for hadn't received the palace protections that Ioannis's few girlfriends and Eleni received.

He and Calla weren't together, yet they'd still run the article insinuating she was trying to infiltrate the royal family.

Infiltrate! Such an ugly word. One that didn't apply to Calla. Besides, who did they want him to wed? No one…and everyone.

"You're making progress, Eleni." Calla beamed as she looked toward Kostas. "I've delivered many babies this way. I suspect three, maybe four, more pushes and the little one will be here. Dr. Kostas, want to catch the baby?"

"Absolutely." Kostas stepped in front of Eleni where the edge of the bed had lowered to aid in the position and shifted so his hands were under Eleni. It was different from anything he'd done, but this was the reason he'd gone into obstetrics.

Caring for women and their children in these first few moments of life was a miracle. The love that appeared on parents' faces when their little ones made their way into this world had gotten him through so many long days. It was his calling, and he'd never considered another specialty.

Delivering his brother's child was a gift he'd never expected, but he was suddenly grateful that Ioannis had called him home.

The contraction started and the room focused on the little one they were waiting for. It took two more pushes, but when a head covered with a mass of dark hair emerged, Kostas looked up at Eleni. "There's a ton of black hair."

His sister-in-law smiled and bore down again. The little princess slipped into Kostas's hands, and he nodded to Eleni. "Your daughter is beautiful."

The queen let out a soft sigh, and a tear slipped down her cheek as her daughter let out a squeal.

Calla helped Eleni lean back in the bed then took the baby from Kostas and laid it on the queen's chest.

"Zelia." Eleni crooned as she kissed the top of her little one's head. She closed her eyes, too focused on the baby to notice the delivery of the placenta.

After a few minutes, Calla tapped Eleni's shoulder and asked if she could clean up the baby. Eleni reluctantly handed the newborn over, and Kostas finished taking care of Eleni.

"She's beautiful." Kostas whispered as he watched Calla wrap the baby.

"Of course she is."

The child cradled in Calla's arms made Kostas's heart ache, but he pushed the desire away. If he was the bad boy of the royal family, and the women he cared for infiltrators, what would someone say of his children? Protecting them from all the camera bulbs, gossip and hurt wouldn't be possible.

"You should take her to Eleni and Ioannis, Uncle Kostas." Calla passed him baby Zelia, and he saw her swallow.

"Congratulations. She is beautiful." Kostas handed the baby to Eleni and watched his brother lean over his wife to stroke his daughter's sweet face.

"Looks just like her momma." Ioannis's voice choked up.

Kostas turned to give the family a few moments. Calla had disappeared, and he couldn't keep the frown from his face. He moved without thinking, his soul needing to find her.

For reasons he didn't want to spend too much time considering.

"Tell Calla thank-you for us." Ioannis's tone was soft. "And tell her I hope the ketchup tastes right soon."

"Oh, my gosh…you ate without me! I knew I

smelled hamburger on your breath. You better have one for me that you can warm up."

"Enjoy your little one." The banter between Ioannis and his wife floated around Kostas, and he was grateful that neither was focused on him.

He needed to find Calla.

Now.

She slipped into the quiet exam room and wrapped her arms around herself as she eyed the ultrasound machine. Calla looked at the door then back at the machine. If she was going to use it, now was the best time.

Kostas was busy with his brother, sister-in-law and new niece. She'd considered taking a pregnancy test, but she'd been so focused on the delivery that she was dehydrated. And she didn't want to wait.

The machine hummed as she flipped it on and grabbed the gel for the ultrasound wand. Pulling the top of her scrubs down, she dropped a sizable dollop of gel on her abdomen and tried to pretend her hand wasn't shaking as she lowered the wand. It took less than thirty seconds for her to confirm what she'd suspected when Ioannis had mentioned Eleni's sudden hatred of clams.

The little bean was moving and shifting on the small screen. She was measuring at nine and half weeks...which matched her time with Kostas perfectly. Tears coated her eyes and her glasses fogged as she watched the movements. "I love you." She whispered the words to her belly as she watched the little one dance on the screen.

No matter what happened next, no matter how Kostas reacted, or anything else, she was certain of one thing. She loved this little one.

Wiping away a tear, she tried to think of what to do next. How was she supposed to tell Kostas? Her bottom lip trembled. If this had happened with Liam, she knew he'd have accused her of trying to trap him.

How would Kostas feel?

Infiltrate the Royal Family... The ugly headline ran through her mind...as did her response to it. That brief statement of certainty uttered less than twenty-four hours ago. How was she supposed to deal with their questions? How was she to protect her child?

She ran her hand along the machine, touching the image and trying to calm herself. She could do this...had to do this. Her child was royal, but that didn't mean anything to Calla. This was her son or daughter. That was all that mattered.

But it would matter to the world.

"Calla..."

She jumped as Kostas's voice echoed in the small room. The ultrasound wand clattered to the ground and the image of her baby disappeared. How had she missed him opening the door?

Pushing the last tear from her cheek, she

reached for the wand and flipped the machine off. This wasn't the way she'd planned to tell him…well, she hadn't known she was pregnant long enough to think of a way, but this would not have made any list.

Putting it off also wasn't an option. Turning, she enfolded her arms at her waist. "Kostas…" Her mouth was dry and she mentally stumbled trying to find the right words to explain what he'd seen.

Kostas seemed frozen in place; the only movement, his mouth that opened and closed several times with no words escaping.

"Kostas," she started again, "it's going to be okay." They were words she wasn't one hundred percent certain of, but she relaxed a little just saying them. She'd find a way. No matter what.

"Are you… Calla…are…" His eyes shifted between the silent ultrasound machine and her.

"Pregnant?" She smiled as she finished his sentence. Then she took a deep breath. It was the moment of truth and she'd handle what came after.

"Yes."

One little word, so tiny, that changed everything.

Kostas ran a hand through his hair then shifted on his heels. "Does our baby look healthy?"

A weight lifted off her shoulders at the simple question. There were no accusations behind it.

Kostas looked surprised, shocked even, but not disappointed.

"It was dancing. I know it doesn't realize it's doing it, but for a second it looked like the little bean was waving." She let out a nervous laugh as she gestured to the screen, as though the image of their spinning child was still on it.

He smiled as he took a step toward her. "Waving?" He looked at her face then down at her belly. "What a sweet thing."

"Do you want to see?" Her hands shook. It was one thing to accept the truth, another to be excited, or happy.

"Yes." He grinned as he grabbed the wand, cleaned it and then picked up the gel. "Do you want to add it?"

The final weight of tension lifted from her as she looked at the happiness on his face.

She couldn't stop the smile spreading across her face as she raised her shirt. "Go ahead."

He dropped the gel on, then immediately moved the wand over her belly. The baby reappeared on the ultrasound screen, and she watched Kostas closely.

A range of emotions cut across his face. Shock, happiness, worry—all things she expected had crossed her features minutes ago.

"So what now?" The question tumbled into the quiet room and her heart flipped. They needed to figure things out, but it didn't have to be right at this moment. They'd had a long day, were both high on emotions from Eleni's delivery and the discovery that they'd be in the same position in eight months.

"We get married."

She laughed. The chuckle echoing in the room as he flipped the ultrasound machine off and handed her a paper towel to wipe off the gel. "You can't be serious."

There were dozens of things he might have stated that wouldn't have shocked her as much as that statement.

Kostas turned, his features anything but jovial. "Yes, Calla. We get married. You're carrying a prince or a princess of Palaío. There is so much that comes with that. So many responsibilities."

"Ones you want to run from! Our child will never sit on the throne of Palaío. Our child will be even farther down the line of succession." The words spilled out; her fears gripping her as she tried to wrap her mind around all that had changed in the last few hours.

Kostas crossed his arms and raised his chin. In this moment, he looked just like the prince he claimed not to want to be. Determined. "You're right that they will never sit on the throne, but they will always be royal. That is something they can never get away from, as I have so clearly demonstrated."

His features softened as he sat beside her on

the exam bed. Maybe it was the exhaustion, or the surprise of finding herself pregnant. Or maybe it was the weeks spent apart from the man she craved to be close to, but Calla couldn't keep her head from leaning against his shoulder.

Kostas wrapped an arm around her and, for just a second, the world felt right. Like this was where she was meant to be. Like everything, even the disastrous five years she'd spent with Liam, had led her here. To Kostas.

"Calla, the baby will be in the line to the throne. I cannot change that. Nor can I change that people will talk, that cameras will chase them. Leaving the island gave me a feeling of freedom, but I dealt with my royalty there too."

He squeezed her tightly. "Anyone they meet will discover the truth and that leads to people wanting to take advantage of them, or desperately seeking to join the fairy tale. I can protect them…and you."

She hadn't wanted the fairy tale, just Kostas. But she knew others who'd have been thrilled to play princess. Hell, the bride Liam had chosen had wanted to join his family because of the prestige of belonging to Seattle "royalty." To a man whose family owned so much property and controlled so many politicians.

Calla had never cared, but that didn't mean people wouldn't think she had. Or treat her child differently because of their status.

And I can't protect them.

It was a truth she didn't want to acknowledge, but it didn't make it less true. She was living in a furnished apartment. After setting aside a sizable portion of her paycheck to repay Liam, she had less than a thousand dollars to her name.

She shuddered and started to move away, but Kostas pulled her into his arms and kissed the top of her head. Her body floated with need for the man.

"Marriage." Calla whispered the word. Kostas could protect their child. Could give them everything Calla couldn't. Her bottom lip trembled. This wasn't how marriage was supposed to work. Wasn't how she'd pictured accepting a proposal...

Though Kostas hadn't proposed. He'd simply stated they would get married. It was too much after the day they'd had. She needed time to figure out her next steps. "I'm going to go home and get some sleep."

She expected him to argue, to demand an answer to his statement. But he let her go.

"Good night, Calla."

She heard the words as she raced from the room, her body letting her flee while her heart screamed for her to race back into his arms.

CHAPTER SEVEN

CALLA ROLLED OVER and looked at the clock. Nearly twelve. She blinked and rubbed her eyes. She hadn't set an alarm after getting home last night. She'd assumed she'd sleep until at least ten, not well past it.

Leaning back in bed, she sighed. For the first time in weeks, she felt rested. Maybe just learning about her pregnancy had been enough to calm her body.

She shook her head…it was the ten hours of sleep that had done it. She rubbed her belly, enjoying a few minutes of quiet, then heard the knocking. Swinging her legs off the bed, she waited for the initial wave of nausea to pass.

Seriously, Calla, how did you miss all the pregnancy signs?

Her nervous laugh echoed in the bedroom as she grabbed her well-worn robe and headed for the door. She was sure Kostas wanted to talk more. And she welcomed the discussion. Last night she'd been too tired and shocked to really discuss his marriage statement. But it was time now.

Flinging open the door, she cinched the top of her robe closed as the well-dressed young woman holding a to-go coffee cup and standing on her doormat smiled at her.

She should have thrown on actual clothes. "I'm sorry. I thought…" Calla cleared her throat. She didn't owe the stranger an explanation for being in a robe in her own home. "Can I help you?"

"I'm Natalia Kilon. Prince Kostas sent me. I think it's best if we talk inside." The young woman stepped through the door as Calla tried to figure out what exactly was going on.

"Excuse me?"

"I'm his assistant." Natalia held out the to-go cup as she smiled at Calla. "It's decaf, but Prince Kostas thought you might like to start the day with coffee."

"He did?" Calla took the cup from the aide and tried to keep her temper in check. It wasn't Natalia's fault that she was here instead of the man she'd expected…and wanted.

"And he figured that I'd want to sleep until after noon?"

"No." Natalia shook her head. "I've been here since just before eight. I've had the palace run me a fresh thermos of coffee every hour since. When noon hit, I waited a bit longer, then just took a chance that you might be awake." She shrugged as though those words made sense. Like requesting a new thermos of decaf coffee and having it delivered to a parking area while waiting for the prince's knocked-up midwife to show signs of life was normal.

Taking a deep breath, Calla offered Natalia a smile. "And where is Kostas?"

"At the clinic. He wanted me to come and see how you were doing."

"But didn't come himself." Fury quickly replaced hurt as she looked at the tall woman standing in her living room.

Natalia either didn't see the anger pulsing through her or didn't react to it. "While most of the press is focused on the birth of Princess Zelia, there are still those who would enjoy breaking the story that Prince Kostas got the nurse from America pregnant. The new royal baby won't stand a chance to that piece of juicy gossip. Even though it won't surprise most of the island that Kostas—" She quickly bit off the last of her sentence. "My apologies ma'am."

"For stating the obvious?" Calla let out a sigh. She knew coming home had been hard for Kostas. He'd been worried about expectations from the moment she'd sat next to him on the plane. And she hated how close her pregnancy was to the rumor that had destroyed his teenage crush. It would cause a scandal when the press learned.

But that did not excuse him from sending an aide to her doorstep.

Color coated Natalia's cheeks as she pulled out a tablet and started hitting her stylus against it. "I think I should start making a list of the things you'd like moved to the palace. I know most of the furniture is rented. I'll ensure that it's sent back to where the clinic got it from. But what items are yours?"

"If you'll give me a minute to get dressed, Natalia?" Calla left before the woman could utter what she assumed would be a polite acceptance.

She pulled on a pair of jeans and glared at the top button. Her jeans still buttoned but they were starting to dig into her barely noticeable bump. Glaring at the ceiling, she shook her head that she'd failed to notice so many things until well past the middle of her first trimester. Reaching into a drawer, she grabbed a hair tie, threaded it through her buttonhole, and secured her jeans that way.

One didn't work with pregnant women for a decade without learning a few tricks!

Dropping an oversized shirt over her head, she slipped on shoes and walked out her front door, saying nothing to Natalia. She wanted to talk to Kostas, and that was what she was going to do.

This issue was between them…period.

It was nearly lunchtime, and the clinic was

quiet as she stepped into the office. Kostas looked up as she closed the door.

"Calla." He nodded but didn't quite meet her gaze.

"Care to explain why there is an aide in my apartment right now?" She crossed her arms as she stood on the other side of the desk.

A knock echoed on the door and Kostas called for entry without even looking at her. Her mouth dropped open as Alexa opened the door. They needed to talk. Now!

"Calla! I didn't know you were here. It's your day off, and Eleni and the baby went home a few hours ago. You should use your free day!"

"Yes, you should," Kostas murmured, but she ignored him.

"I needed to see to a few things. Get something straightened out, then I am leaving...promise." She addressed Alexa, but she meant the words for Kostas. She was not leaving until they talked.

"Well, Kali and I are going to grab lunch at the bistro down the block. We don't have another patient until almost two. So—" she flicked her gaze to Kostas "—unless you need something, Dr. Drakos?"

"Enjoy your lunch, Alexa."

She was gone and Calla rounded on Kostas. "Explain. Now."

Kostas rolled his head and let out a yawn. As the primary OBGYN in the capital, he didn't get many off days. No way to sleep until nearly noon after a long delivery. She wanted to grant him some slack, and probably would, if he'd just meet her gaze.

"It's safer for Natalia to be at your apartment. Once the news breaks that you are pregnant and we are getting married, your life is going to change. In ways that you cannot imagine yet. I wanted to give you a few more days of relative normalcy."

"By sending a stranger to ask me what I'd like to take with me? A stranger to ask me what to box and what to leave behind? Before we've even had a chance to talk?" Her body shook with emotion, but he still wouldn't meet her eyes. Last night he'd held her so tightly. Looked so excited, shocked but excited, to discover that she was pregnant. But now...

Had a night of rest made him rethink the statement of marriage? It hurt more than she wanted to acknowledge, but she couldn't really blame him. A night of passion had resulted in so many life-altering changes. However they felt about each other, they were tied together forever by the little one she carried.

"We don't have to marry, Kostas. Many people co-parent without walking down the aisle." The words tasted terrible as she uttered them. She didn't want him to marry her for the baby. But she was drawn to the man, felt like she was where she was meant to be when she was in his arms.

That didn't mean they'd make a good long-term match, though.

"We are getting married, Calla."

Such certainty. Like an order from the prince he claimed to hate being. She felt her nose twitch as she watched him.

He made a few more notes on the page before him and she lost the bit of her temper she was still controlling.

"I am not marrying a man who won't even look up from his work at me. A man who is embarrassed by who he got pregnant." The angry words spilled out, yet it was the sob at the end that nearly broke her. It wasn't fair to make such an accusation, but he was a prince, and she really was just the knocked-up midwife.

The palace staff was too well trained to say it to her face, but others... The headlines, the questions about her status—they were inevitable. It had been one thing for Liam to point out, but for an entire island nation to question her, to judge her...

Calla wrapped her arms around herself and forced the fear and worry away. There wasn't time; and she was not weak. She was a strong woman, a soon-to-be mother who would do anything to protect her child. With or without Kostas, she'd ensure their child never questioned that

Calla loved them for who they were as a person. Not the title their birth afforded them.

She reached for the door handle, ready to storm back to her apartment and tell Natalia to get out. That she wasn't going anywhere.

Kostas's dark eyes landed on her. His mouth fell open. "Embarrassed by who you are? I don't care who you are. It's you who didn't want to date a royal. Who's trapped by fate now?"

The desperation in his voice stilled her feet.

He stood, walked toward her, stopping just inches from her. "Despite your clear aversion to dating a royal, putting distance between us... Despite everything, I cannot stop looking out for you. Listening to the fluctuations of your voice so I know when you are happy, stressed, tired."

He pushed a hand through his hair as he looked at her. "Last night, when you leaned your head against me, I desperately wanted you. Still want you."

Kostas took a deep breath. "I wanted to be there when you woke up this morning. But I also want to protect you, and I know how hard that is going to be. It is safer for you, and for our child, if no one suspects anything at all until you are safely in my rooms at the palace. But all I can do is think of you, dream of you, look out for you."

The air in the room felt too thick to breathe.

Calla laid a hand on Kostas's heart. It was beating rapidly under her fingers. "Kostas..."

There were so many things she should say. So many things they still needed to address, but her soul refused to voice those in this moment.

She rose on her toes and brushed her lips against his. His arms wrapped around hers. Tightening as he deepened the kiss. The world shifted just as it had the night they'd first met. Everything clicked into place.

Kostas broke the kiss but kept her close to his body, like he wasn't ready to let her go. Calla sighed, enjoying the heat coming off him. The subtle scent of clean laundry and Kostas that she'd craved for so long.

"I've missed you." His words were soft as his fingers stroked her back. "So much."

"Me too." Calla hugged him tightly. Then she made herself start the conversation they both seemed to be putting off.

"We have chemistry." She laid a hand over her belly. "But marriage is a big deal, Kostas. A forever deal. At least, the version of it I want."

She stepped out of his arms. If she didn't put a bit of distance between them, she'd lose the smidgen of courage she'd worked up for this.

"You're carrying a royal baby, Calla."

"I am." That was a truth she couldn't escape. He might wish he was just Dr. Drakos, but that wasn't life. Their child was going to carry the title of prince or princess. Their childhood would look completely different from hers.

Still, she wouldn't cheat any child out of a loving family. "Chemistry doesn't mean we are meant to be together, though. A marriage of convenience—" Calla barely caught the laugh in the back of her throat. "This isn't a historical romance. This is our life. We get to decide."

"Marriage to me protects the baby. Ensures the entire weight of Ioannis's authority comes to his or her aid if needed," Kostas countered.

"And it won't, if we aren't married?" Calla shifted on her feet; her body aching to lean into Kostas but needing confirmation of this first.

Kostas blinked. "What?"

"If we aren't married and something happens with our son or daughter; if they need something, the palace will deny them because we didn't marry?"

"I…" Kostas opened his mouth and shut it. "I…"

"So?" Calla raised a brow as she kissed his cheek. She knew Ioannis and Eleni wouldn't deny their child the protections of the palace. His father may have refused to come to the aid of his second born, but his brother was in charge now. "Why don't we take a bit of time, get to know each other? Date."

"The press—"

"Will come for me when they find out about the pregnancy anyway. But until we are sure about marriage, we can keep this very discreet."

She inhaled a deep breath. She didn't want to be his secret, but she knew once the press learned of their relationship...her stomach twisted at the thought of press at her door. But she'd navigate it. Life was too short to accept a person for convenience. "My parents loved each other. It was a gift. Something that carried them through their lowest of lows and highest of highs. Maybe I didn't grow up with every luxury, but my home was happy and filled with love."

Calla paused briefly before continuing. "I won't accept less than that. My child—our child—deserves to see their parents love each other."

"Royal marriages don't have a great history with love." His tone was so bitter, her heart ached for him. That belief was rooted deep, and she knew of his mother's struggles. But what about Ioannis and Eleni?

"Says the man who watched his brother, the King of Palaío, fawn over his wife yesterday. Who cooed with his newborn daughter and rubbed his queen's back."

"They are the exception."

"Maybe. But our child deserves to see that, too, whether it's between us or..." Her brain caught the words as she imagined Kostas with another. It hurt, even in her imagination, but this was a point she needed to make.

"Between us or other future partners we have. I will not deprive them of that for some royal pro-

tocol issue." Calla bit her lip. "If you aren't interested in seeing if what we have is more than
just passion—"

"Yes," he interjected. "Yes, I am interested."
He crossed his arms, uncrossed them, crossed
them again and then reached for her hands. "But
with some ground rules, to protect you and the
baby."

She squeezed his hand. Ground rules sounded
a lot like control, but she was determined not to
give in to the baggage she carried from Liam.
This would be different; she'd see to it, or she'd
walk away.

Kostas laid his free hand on her belly and the
hand in hers rubbed the base of her wrist. "We
meet in secret, at least for now. That means no
trips to your apartment or the palace. You keep
palace security on speed dial in your phone, and
if something threatens our child, we move you to
the security of the palace. *Immediately.*"

Secret meetings. Why did that sound so different from her statement of discreet? Calla swallowed. It wasn't ideal, but it was better than a
marriage of convenience. At least for now. "Any
other requirements, Prince Kostas?"

His hand dropped hers and raised to her face.
He stroked her cheek. "We find time for each
other, each day. Even if it is only ten minutes.

I've gone weeks with distance between us. I don't want that again."

"That's the easiest thing to say yes to." Calla tipped up on her toes and kissed him. They felt right together, and they owed each other the chance to see if this was the place they were meant to be. And they owed their child a happy home, even if it meant their parents weren't together.

Though Calla's heart refused to accept the possibility her brain offered.

Kostas paced the small balcony on The Grotto, his eyes trained on the trees and ridgeline for any indications of cameras or visitors that should not be in the area. The Grotto was a secure location…mostly because it was a rarely used hideaway in the mountains.

Baby Zelia's birth had captured the nation's attention, but when word broke that another royal was on the way… The bad boy's baby, conceived with a foreign nurse out of wedlock.

The headlines his mother and Maria had faced would look like puff pieces compared to such a revelation. Kostas pulled his hand over his face at the questions that would be thrown at Calla.

And he wanted to protect her from every single sling. Wanted to wrap the weight of the palace around her to ensure no slights ever touched her. His mother hadn't felt protected. His teen-age crush's concerns had simply been ignored, his pleas for aid falling on his father's deaf ears. Calla would never feel that way. He'd make sure of it.

She'd never deal with a lie or overstatement. He'd push back. He doubted Ioannis would mind, but if he did…well, Kostas planned to do it any-way. Calla would always feel protected…always.

Kostas breathed in the mountain air, forcing himself to focus on finally having Calla to himself again. Finally getting to spend time with-out worrying if anyone saw or suspected. Their first date!

Or was it their second date? Did they count the diner in Dayton with cheap burgers and salty fries?

"You have quite the pondering look on your face, Kostas."

Calla's voice caught him off guard. He'd not seen her hike in on the back trail. That meant he could have missed others. He scanned the hori-zon one more time then turned to her.

He dropped his lips to her cheek and his heart settled as her scent floated over him. Calla was here. She was safe, and so was their baby. That was all that mattered.

"How did you get here? I was monitoring the main trail." He pushed a lock of dark hair behind her ear, his fingers unable to keep from reaching for her.

"Land trail." She pointed to the edge of the property, "It was one option on the very detailed sheet Natalia emailed me this afternoon. It looked like the easiest route from my apartment. And it's lit almost all the way back down the trailhead. Still…" She held up a flashlight before setting it on the small table.

Calla stepped closer and slid her fingers through his. He hoped it was because she couldn't keep her hands from him, either.

"So why were you looking so pensively into the trail? Scouting wayward cameras?" Her giggle hovered around them.

He knew she was trying to make light of the situation, but she needed to look for cameras. Or do like he did and just assume that they were always trained on him. If he never broke the princely expectations foisted on him in public, then people couldn't complain. Or at least they couldn't complain as much.

Rather than give a lecture she was likely to hear from the protocol office ad nauseam after she was publicly linked to him, he offered the other truth. "I was trying to figure out if this was our first or second date? Does the diner count?"

"Of course it counts." Calla's eyes widened as she held his gaze. "It's why we are here! Why…"

Her hand dropped to her belly before she smiled. "It was definitely our first date."

"I like to think we'd have ended up here, even if we hadn't had the medical crisis on our flight." The hope floated into the early evening and he pulled her close. "Like to believe that you'd have landed in the clinic and our connection would have been too much to ignore at some point."

Even if I was royal. But would I have set aside a space in my heart if we hadn't met before? Kostas wanted to believe their initial connection was strong enough, but he wasn't sure. And he hated that.

Her lips twitched and her mouth opened, but whatever words initially hovered there, she swallowed as she looked over his shoulder at the retreat. Perhaps the same thoughts were floating through her mind.

"So, where are we?"

Rather than push, Kostas wrapped his arm around her and led her into the retreat. "This is The Grotto. It's a retreat my father created then rarely used. My brother updated a few rooms, but I think there are bathrooms that still have pink tile that was in fashion in the 1950s. My father planned to fully renovate it but..." Kostas shrugged.

This had been his father's place, his hideaway. On the few occasions he had come here with his mother, Ioannis and Kostas hadn't accompanied them.

"Your father?" Calla leaned her head against his as they moved into the retreat. "I'm not sure I've ever heard you mention him."

Kostas let out a small grunt. "That's because there is little to say. My father was 'the King.' Always. He was a husband and a father after caring for the country. Maybe that was the right choice, but it left little room for the rest of us. He ceded control of the throne to Ioannis only when the stroke he had made it impossible for him to carry on. He died a few weeks later. Without being king, I am not sure he had much to live for."

Calla squeezed the arm she had around his center. "That sounds hard."

"It was." Kostas bit the inside of his cheek as emotion wrapped through him. This was a heavy topic for a second date…but maybe it was best she knew. "My father wanted to control everything."

He let out a breath and shook his head. "Actually, my father did control everything. If it didn't benefit the crown, it didn't get mentioned or addressed. It's why Mom left."

"So he would have had thoughts about our relationship."

"Undoubtedly," Kostas confirmed. His father would have hated that both his sons had gotten women pregnant out of wedlock. Would have attempted to control that narrative as soon as he'd learned it. His mother...

Kostas's heart seized as he thought of his mom. And her reaction to being a grandmother. She'd died so young, but he knew she'd have loved that stage of her life.

His mother wouldn't have cared that they'd gotten pregnant out of wedlock. Wouldn't have cared that Calla was a foreigner; that she didn't have a title. All that would have mattered was the smile she brought to her son's face. "My mom wouldn't have cared, though. She'd have thought you were perfect."

Perfect for me.

Calla's lips twisted down and pulled back. "I'm hardly perfect. The best I can hope for is delightfully flawed." Her nose twitched as she looked around the retreat living room. "I love the windows overlooking the mountains here. I bet it's lovely first thing in the morning."

"It is. And at sunset, which we'll see in about two hours." He pulled her to him. "What do you mean by 'delightfully flawed'? That is an..." he hesitated "...interesting combination of words. Did your parents say that?"

"Oh, no!" Calla laughed, but the sound was uncomfortable. "Liam, my ex, always called me that. We dated for five years, got engaged, but I didn't meet his family's expectations. I got so used to saying it for years that it still slips out."

A person she cared for; someone she'd considered spending her life with, had called her "delightfully flawed" so often it still slipped into conversation? That was horrible.

"Is he why you're here?"

He was so glad she was in Palaío, but had she been running from an ex? Her past didn't matter to him, but he wanted to know everything about the woman before him.

"In a roundabout way. He helped me pay for nursing school and when we broke up…well, he wanted the money back. It would cost more in lawyers to fight than repay. I've nearly paid it off and I'm here because the pay from your lovely clinic lets me clear the last bit off within a year."

"He wanted you to repay him?" Kostas knew his mouth was hanging open, but he couldn't help it. What a callous thing to do at the end of a relationship.

She squeezed his hand as she stepped to the window overlooking the hills. "Liam…" She hesitated, and Kostas didn't push. He wanted to know, to understand, but he wouldn't force it.

"He probably would've gotten along well with your father. He was quite controlling. I didn't realize it as quickly as I should have. But I did my best to fit the cast he and his family wanted. Blond…society fiancée, but it was never enough."

She shrugged. "And I'm glad. I am much happier being me than trying to fit someone else's mold. I won't do that again!"

Calla clapped. "But as soon as I pay off Liam, I can kick my final tie to him. Heavy stuff for date two!" She grinned and looked for the kitchen.

"The baby and I are hungry. What are you feeding us?"

She was ready to change the topic. He understood, but he couldn't stop the bead of anger pooling in his belly on her behalf. So her ex had helped her get her degree then demanded repayment when she didn't measure up to his parents' expectations? What had those expectations been that Calla couldn't meet them?

He'd called her perfect a few times, and he still felt the word fit her. Rationally, he knew no one was perfect, but Calla was caring, intelligent, beautiful, brave...what else could one want?

He made a note to have Natalia track down Liam and the loan. Preferably without Calla knowing. He'd have it paid off and perhaps send along a note thanking the man for his stupidity. After all, it had led Calla to him.

He'd surprise Calla with the news when it was done. His gift to her, a true gift, one he never expected repayment for.

"We're having moussaka." The palace cook had placed the spiced meat dish, layered with eggplant and tomato sauce, in the warmer this afternoon and he'd driven it up with him. "And there's *kourabiedes* for dessert."

"Ooh, butter cookies! I love those!" Her eyes sparkled as she pointed to the hallway. "Kitchen this way?"

Kostas took her hand and kissed the top of it. "Can't let you and the baby go hungry. Follow me, my lady."

"My lady!" Calla laughed, and the sound was relaxed. Not the nervous laugh he hated to hear come from her sweet lips. "I could get used to that phrase."

He squeezed her hand as he led her to the kitchen. If she enjoyed hearing "my lady," how would she feel when people referred to her as "Your Highness" or "Princess"? Hopefully, with the same bubbly enthusiasm he'd just witnessed.

"So now that you've fed me, what's next?" Calla grinned as Kostas put the rest of their dinner in the fridge. She hopped up on the counter just like she'd done at home for years.

Kostas turned and looked at her. For a moment, she almost hopped off. Liam had hated this habit, but she'd never managed to break it.

As a young girl, her father had placed her on the edge of the counter so she could watch her parents cook. She did it without thinking.

Rather than comment on her position, Kostas stood in front of her. His eyes burned with desire.

He held her gaze before his attention dropped to where their child was growing.

"You are gorgeous. And now that you're sated, what would you like to do?" His voice was sultry, and her body hummed as its cord raked across her.

She wrapped her legs around him and pulled him closer as her arms circled his neck. She'd trapped him—though he looked like he had no intention of going anywhere. His breath caught as she lightly kissed his lips. It would be so easy to fall into bed with him, to whisper that she wanted him to carry her to bed. To lose herself in his arms.

Part of her wanted to. Cried out for her to beg him to touch her. But she also wanted, craved, more than just a physical connection to him. She brushed her lips against his then pulled back.

He let her pull away, but his palms rested on her knees.

"What movie options are there? If this was a second date between two regular people, we might go to the big screen. Pay too much for popcorn and sodas, and think about holding hands in the dark."

Kostas chuckled. "'Think about holding hands in the dark'? That sounds more like a teen romcom." He kissed her cheek as he lifted her off the counter and then pulled her toward a door on the left.

He swung it open with flair and she covered her mouth as he flipped on the lights. She'd heard people discuss their home theaters. Known men to brag about putting in a large screen, but this... this was basically a small theater.

She blinked as she looked at the seats—or rather, couches. Designed for comfort and cuddles. The popcorn maker in the corner was only a little smaller than the one in the theater by her house.

"The bathrooms may still have pink tile, but Ioannis upgraded the theater, my lady." He winked as he walked over to the popcorn machine, flipped it on and dumped the kernels in, then looked at her. "We've got a huge library of movies. And I also have most of the streaming services, so rom-coms, drama, comedy? What's your favorite?"

The smell of popcorn started to fill the space as she looked at the place. So this was what dating a prince was like!

"Most of the streaming services? Including the ones from the States?" She crossed her arms as the request built in her chest.

Kostas seemed to sense her hesitation. "Yep. So what is it you're craving? A talk show, reality television, baking show?"

He was so far off.

"You ever seen the ridiculous History channel show *Ancient Aliens*?" Calla felt heat flood her cheeks. "My dad and I watched it together and it's hilarious."

Kostas ran his hand through his short hair.

"Do you miss your longer hair?" Calla ran her hand along the shortened length. "I liked it. Not that the short hair doesn't look nice too."

He blinked, clearly confused by the turn of subject, which she couldn't blame him for. "Are you trying to change topics now because we can get any show in the world on a big screen, with a bucket of popcorn from an actual popcorn machine? And you want to watch a show about how aliens helped ancient people build things... a show that history can easily debunk but is like an accident you can't look away from?"

He kissed her cheek as she felt happiness bloom inside her. "You've seen it!"

"Only a few episodes. Well, almost every episode."

"So you did have a weird thing besides silly mugs. Oh, Alexa would love to know this."

"But you'll keep my secret, right?" He kissed her, lingering for a few seconds.

"I would have agreed without the kiss. But that was nice." Calla grinned as she leaned into him and kissed him again. "Besides, I couldn't out this secret without outing my love of it too.

He brushed his lips against hers again then handed her a bowl and scoop. "You get the popcorn ready; I'll go load up the show."

Calla watched him walk to the small room off the theater and let out a sigh. She was dating a prince, and everything was different, but in this moment, in this one perfect piece of time, it just felt like that first night. Like they were Calla and Kostas.

The lights and questions would come, but they'd find a way to navigate it together.

CHAPTER EIGHT

"GOOD MORNING, CALLA." Kostas's voice was light as he slid his stuff into the small locker next to hers.

"Morning, Kostas." She couldn't keep the grin off her face. They'd spent the last few nights at The Grotto, watching old movies and silly alien documentaries. While working, they kept things professional, but if anyone walked into the employee lounge at the moment, she bet they'd suspect the truth.

She was happy. Really happy with Kostas. He made her feel seen. Whether it was when they cooked some of the dishes she'd learned at her parents' side or watching ridiculous documentaries, she never felt like she had to be more than who she was.

After years of agonizing over what she was wearing, how she spoke, how she held herself, it was a joy to just be herself. And made her realize how unhappy she'd been with Liam. Once she finished repaying the loan, she vowed to never think of the man again.

"How did you sleep?" His voice was low. It was a question meant to check in on her and the baby. One that he didn't want to risk the rest of the office hearing.

She was sleeping better than she'd been before. But last night she'd tossed and turned. Not with worry, though.

No matter what time they got done at The Grotto, he walked her to the top of the trailhead, then watched until she got into the car she'd parked with the others. It was sweet, but she craved more than the kisses he left on her lips.

She wanted him in her bed. Wanted to wake up next to him. To sip coffee with him, even if hers was decaf.

"Not as well as I would have liked."

He arched a brow. But before she added a suggestive statement, Alexa opened the locker room door.

"Dr. Drakos!" The panic in her voice was unmistakable, and Calla turned to see what was wrong, all thoughts of convincing Kostas to spend the night with her flying away.

"Adrian called. Myra is in labor. She requested a home birth, but Adrian says she's been laboring for too long. I couldn't get him to give me more information."

"This is their first." Kostas pursed his lips.

"But Myra's mother was a midwife and she helped with dozens of births. She knows what to expect."

"I think her mother always expected she'd go into medicine, but its numbers that really make her happy," Alexa added, looking at Calla. "Still, Adrian isn't usually overly excitable."

"His wife is having their first baby, but maybe we should go out. If she's in labor, Calla and I will be there for the home delivery, anyway. I can come back to the clinic if we have any other expectant mothers needing delivery."

Calla opened the locker and grabbed the backpack she'd dropped into it just a minute before.

The door to Myra and Adrian's small house opened as Calla raised her hand. Myra looked exhausted and more than a little ticked as she tilted her head, shifting her gaze between Calla and Kostas. "So Adrian's worried self got you two out here before necessary." She cringed, grabbed her belly and breathed through the contraction.

Keeping her mouth closed, Calla monitored Myra's breathing and took stock of the mother's appearance. She looked tired, but that was to be expected. The contractions were clearly painful, but not debilitating. All good signs.

"You've been having contractions since one o'clock." Adrian's words carried over his wife, who grunted but either didn't or couldn't offer a rebuttal.

One a.m. put Myra at just over nine hours of labor. Not a terribly long time for a first-time mother. Though Myra might feel differently as the person currently experiencing the pains.

The contraction ended, and she threw her head up to the ceiling as she sucked in a long breath. "There was no need to send for anyone yet. As I've said repeatedly, Adrian. The contractions are still only six minutes apart. My water is intact—" The words left Myra's lips and she immediately looked down.

Water pooled under her bare feet as she let out a curse under her breath. Her cheeks flushed as she met Calla's gaze. "He will never stop talking about this. You know that, right?"

"I do." Calla nodded. "But now that your water has broken, I guess it's a good thing we are here."

Adrian's grin was brilliant behind his wife, but he wisely kept his mouth shut as she moved to the side to let them in.

"Contractions are six minutes apart?" Kostas asked as he stepped into the small living room.

"They are," Myra confirmed. "I'm going to change into something less wet." She waddled off, still not looking at her husband.

"How long do you think she'll stay mad at me?" Adrian crossed then uncrossed his arms as he looked toward the hallway where his wife had disappeared.

Kostas stepped up beside him and dropped the midwifery bag with all their supplies. Offering Adrian a comforting smile, he shrugged. "Many women are mad at their significant others during labor. There is a reason it's a standard storyline in comedy shows."

"I guess. At least her snarls aren't as deep or cutting as her mother's." Adrian let out a laugh before sharing a knowing glance with Kostas.

Clearly, there was a story there Calla missed as an outsider. She raised a brow, and Adrian chuckled. "Leta, my mother-in-law, doesn't think I'm good enough for her daughter. She's quieted down about it now, but—"

"She wouldn't have been happy with anyone," Myra stated as she rounded the corner.

"Maybe a prince." Adrian grinned as his pregnant wife came to his side.

"Well, Ioannis is taken, and the rebel prince over here would have gotten an even rougher time than you. Titled or not." Color invaded her cheeks as she looked at Kostas. "No offense, Dr. Drakos. I…"

Calla opened her mouth, looking for the right words to defend Kostas. To playfully state that the man was as far from that reputation as possible. Hell, it was her putting the brakes on the marriage he'd suggested when she'd found out she was pregnant.

But before she could say anything, Kostas waved it off. "None taken, Myra." He offered them each a smile. It was only the twitch in his hand that let Calla know the words had landed close to his heart.

Reminded him once more that it wasn't really him people saw, but a caricature. That, despite the years away from the island, completing med school and then returning when the island needed him, the reputation earned unfairly in his youth still clung to him.

"Do you have the water bath ready?" Calla hoped the question redirected the awkwardness of the room back to the reason they were all there.

"Yes. It's out here." Adrian gestured for Kostas to follow him while Calla waited with Myra.

Another contraction started and she breathed through it then started pacing. "I know my mother wasn't thrilled that I married Adrian. Thought that he was beneath me since I got my master's degree and he's a carpenter." She rubbed her lower back as she walked from one side of the small living room to the other.

Calla didn't interrupt. She'd heard all sorts of tales since she'd started her career. Something about labor brought out the chattiness in some of her patients. Maybe it was wanting to drop old baggage as new life entered the world. Or perhaps it just passed the time while mothers worked through the long hours it typically took to bring forth new life.

"But he makes me laugh. And he makes the most beautiful furniture." She sucked in a deep breath.

A tear slipped down her cheek. "I can't explain it. Maybe on the outside we don't look like we should click. A mathematician and a carpenter, but he's my person. It's just that simple. Adrian is my person. Does that sound ridiculous?"

Kostas stuck his head back in the room. "Everything still okay in here? We're filling the water bath. In a few minutes, if you want to sit in it, it might give you a bit of relief."

His eyes flicked just briefly to Calla and her heart swelled with emotion. Her person. Maybe it really was as simple and as uncomplicated as that. Adrian was Myra's match…and Kostas was hers.

"No, that doesn't sound ridiculous," Calla murmured, but Myra was bent over in the throes of another contraction.

"Sorry, what did you say?" Myra wiped the back of her hand across her forehead as the contraction ended. That one was not six minutes apart.

"Nothing." Calla grinned.

* * *

"Are you okay?" Calla's voice startled him in the quiet dark of their walk back to the clinic. A clinic staffer had picked up all their gear and taken their dirty scrubs while they'd waited with Myra and Adrian for the local pediatrician to check in on the newborn.

It had been a long but wonderful day…mostly.

"Of course." The words carried through the night, and he wished he felt he could hold her hand. The last two weeks, they'd made time for each other like they'd promised. But it was always at The Grotto, or in the quiet times when they were the only ones at the clinic.

The times when he knew for sure they were alone. It was the right choice, but he envied others. Other couples walked home together, arms linked, head on shoulders. No worries about it making headlines. Just able to enjoy the moments together without realizing what a special gift that actually was.

As if she'd read his mind, Calla reached for him. The pressure of her touch sent calmness floating through him. Then concern as he tracked the empty pathway in front of them.

He squeezed her palm and pulled away. Until she was ready to move into the safety of the palace, until he could fully protect her, he wouldn't risk anything.

"Adrian and Myra's baby is adorable." Her whisper carried in the evening air.

"She is. And Adrian will never let her forget we were there just as her water broke."

"And Myra will not let him forget that she didn't deliver for another six hours." Calla laughed.

The sound sent a thrill through him. He could hear the brilliant smile attached to it. A happy Calla, a safe Calla, was the most important thing to him. He'd had a realization today, though. He understood Adrian's panic.

Understood why the man had gone against his partner's wishes to ensure she and their child were safe. Despite all the evidence before him, they were fine.

For years, Kostas had watched nervous partners pace the halls, worry running through their features. Even when labor was progressing normally, the partner not delivering the child carried an anxiety through the entire process. Kostas hadn't planned on having children...but he'd always prided himself that he knew too much to worry over nothing.

Pride... He mentally scoffed at how little he'd really known. Heck, if Calla would let him ensconce her in the palace for the next several months so he could ensure nothing bad happened to her, he'd order it done tonight.

Six months ago, he'd have assured himself that

he knew too much about delivery, understood the risks that needed worry and those that were just part of the process to be concerned if he ever found a life partner.

Now he'd side with Adrian. Rationally, he knew Myra was right. They hadn't needed to call for a midwife for at least another two hours. But the idea of Calla in pain, walking the halls for hours, cringing in agony, sent shudders through his soul.

The clinic came into view and he slowed his pace, not yet wanting to say goodbye.

"Why don't you come to my place? We can make dinner…a very late dinner." Calla bumped his hip with hers.

The refusal hung on his tongue. There were hundreds of reasons to say no. To protect Calla and their child. If anyone saw him at her place…

Before he could say anything, she offered, "I need dinner despite the late hour. You're hungry too. I heard your stomach growl. Besides, it's nearly midnight. No one will see you, and you can sneak out early before anyone else is awake.

"Don't say no." She grabbed his hands and pulled him to the path up to her apartment. "Come home with me, Kostas."

He wanted to hesitate—to think through everything. But his feet seemed to have a mind of their own.

"You aren't the rebel, Kostas." Calla squeezed

his hand as they walked together. "I know that you worry about what happens when people learn about us. You aren't the stereotype. Myra was joking."

"She was." His voice sounded hoarse. He wanted to blame the late hour but...

"But the words still hurt." Calla pulled the key to her apartment out of her bag with her free hand.

He wished he could say they didn't. Wished that after all these years, it didn't bother him. That he'd developed an impenetrable skin. "She didn't mean anything by them."

The door to her apartment swung open and Kostas inhaled and let the worries pass him by. "And tonight, or what's left of it, I just want to enjoy my time with you."

Kostas dropped a kiss on her lips. She leaned into him, her body molding to his. This was his happy place.

"Calla..." He wanted to take her to bed. To lift her in his arms, carry her to her room, then spend the night lost in her arms. But they needed sustenance.

The clinic wasn't open on Sunday, so they had the day off. Assuming no mothers went into labor. He had all night. And he'd make sure he was gone before the rest of the world was awake.

"I have leftovers in the fridge." She kissed his

cheek. "Leftovers that we can enjoy cold, so we can go to bed." The heat in her eyes burned him.

"Sorry, I forgot the other kitchen chair was broken. I meant to tell the landlord, but since it's only me…" She shrugged as she hopped off the kitchen counter and grabbed his empty plate.

"I think you like sitting on the counter." Kostas slid behind her at the sink, wrapping his arms around her waist as she ran the warm water over the dishes.

He dropped his lips to the base of her neck and barely contained a moan of need as her butt rubbed into him. The month of distance, the weeks of pent-up need barreled through him as her body moved against him. But he would not rush this.

Calla turned in his arms, wrapping her arms around his neck. "Kostas…"

He drew circles with his fingers lightly on her back as her head tilted up to his. Her lips beckoned and he skimmed his mouth along her jaw, grazing her skin before finally claiming her lips.

She sighed and opened her mouth. His hands slipped to her waist and he pulled her tightly to him as their tongues danced. His senses were nearly overwhelmed as heat consumed him.

Calla pulled back, running her hand along his jaw. "Come to bed?"

"Lead the way."

Her eyes lit up and she grabbed his hand. The apartment was small, and he was grateful that it took only seconds to work their way to her bedroom. He flicked on the bedside light. After weeks apart, he wanted to see her.

Needed to see her reactions to his touch.

She pulled his shirt over his head, dropping it to the floor. Her fingers trailed along his skin and his body ached for her.

"Calla." Her name sounded like a prayer as it escaped his lips. "Sweetheart." He cupped her cheeks with his hands, dropping a light kiss to her lips before slipping his fingers under her light shirt.

He sighed as her shirt dropped to the ground, then grinned as he saw the ponytail holder looping through her buttonhole.

"I know it looks silly—" Calla shrugged "—but it works."

Laying his hand on her lower belly, he kissed her again. "You're perfect." He captured her mouth once more before she could argue with him. She was perfect to him, and he wanted her to hear that so much that she never doubted it.

His fingers unwrapped the makeshift waist extender, and he pushed the pants down her hips. He unclipped her bra and smiled as he rubbed a thumb over one nipple then the other.

She rocked her hips toward him. "My breasts are sensitive."

"You'll tell me if it's too much, promise?" Kostas trailed kisses along the top of her breasts, his body screaming for him to claim her.

"I meant…" Her eyes dilated with pleasure as she looked at him. "I meant I want you to touch me." Her hand grabbed his, guiding him back to her breasts, showing him exactly how she wanted him to love her.

It was erotic, and he loved ceding to her wishes. However Calla wanted pleasure, he'd give it to her! He circled her nipples with his fingers, watching the need play across her face.

Lowering his head, he suckled each of her nipples then carefully guided her to the bed. Her skin felt velvety under his fingers as he lowered her to the mattress. He quickly stripped off the final pieces of his clothing and lay next to her on the bed, pulling her into his arms.

Her backside rubbed against him, and he nipped at the nape of her neck. "I want you, Calla. So badly. But I won't rush this."

Leaning her head back, she kissed him. Her hand stroked his thigh, desperately close to his manhood, and desire nearly overwhelmed him.

Feathering stokes down her body, he touched her heat, loving the moan echoing in the room as he pressed her bud. Wrapping his other arm under her, he grazed his thumb across her nipples, matching the motion of each hand. It was a delicate dance to bring Calla pleasure, and as she arched against him, he trailed his tongue down her beautiful body.

Her hips moved on their own against his fingers. "Kostas…" Her voice cracked as her body shuddered.

There was nothing he'd ever enjoyed more than hearing his name on her lips as he brought her to orgasm.

"Kostas, I need you." Her heady plea hung in the air as she brought her mouth to his. She seized him as she rolled on top of him.

"All of you." Her eyes glittered as she held him with her hands.

Kostas barely fought off the urge to drive into her as she slowly lowered her body on his. "Calla!"

"Does it feel good?" She feathered kisses across his jaw as she rose nearly off him again.

"Yes…" he breathed as she started the slow motion again, her eyes watching his every move. He hissed as she rose once more before fully taking him…again.

"Calla…now. Please."

As soon as the words left his lips, she eased the rest of the way down. He gripped her waist as she rocked them both into oblivion then collapsed against him.

"Nice to know I can make you beg too." Her words were light as she lay on him.

Kostas wrapped his arms around her. "Never doubt that I want you, sweetheart. So much."

The alarm he'd set buzzed and Kostas stretched, enjoying the warmth of Calla next to him. He tapped the icon on his phone, glad that he'd remembered to put it under his pillow so he wouldn't wake her.

He glared at the still dark window. He didn't want to head out. It was a simple realization with so much power behind it.

He'd suggested marriage when he'd learned she was pregnant. It was the most pragmatic way to protect her. A job he swore he'd do better than his father.

They enjoyed each other's company. There was passion between them. That was more of a connection than so many royal couples experienced. Despite the modern era, arranged marriages in the aristocracy and wealthy classes were much more common than anyone wanted to admit. It wasn't confined to the waste bin of history; it just wasn't talked about.

Kostas had figured that he and Calla would make a good match. But it was more than that. He wanted her next to him every night. He ran a hand along her hip before draping it over her belly. There was a slight bump there. One no one would notice but that hinted at how their life was going to change.

A smile spread on his face as he ran a thumb along where the child rested. Or maybe danced while their parents rested. Soon, Calla would know, and in a few months, Kostas would feel it too.

Kostas couldn't wait.

He kissed her cheek and she rolled into his arms, leaning her head against his shoulder. Kostas looked at the clock: just after four in the morning. He needed to leave soon, but he could hold her for a few more minutes.

CHAPTER NINE

"KOSTAS?"

Calla's voice hovered above him in the dream. His body felt heavy, like he couldn't quite make his feet move. He frowned as he reached for something...or tried to. But his hands came up empty.

"Kostas?"

He turned again. Looking for Calla. His heart raced as he looked into the void but couldn't find her. He needed to reach her. Needed to protect her.

"Kostas."

This time his eyes shot open and he blinked as Calla grinned. She was wearing a well-worn blue robe that hit just above her knees. It was loosely tied, and he could tell she wore nothing under it.

It was the type of getup longtime lovers wore when they were comfortable around each other. The kind that wasn't designed to be sexy...though anything Calla wore would make his mouth water. Maybe it was just what she'd thrown on, but part of him wanted to believe it was because she was comfortable with him.

It is the best way to start a morning. The thought registered against his brain as he sat up, looking to the window where daylight peaked out from under her curtain.

"I overslept."

"You did," Calla confirmed as she handed him the mug of coffee. "I made you a pot of regular coffee. That is an act of…" Her voice paused as she looked at him.

His ears perked up as he looked at her. Part of him wanted so badly to hear her say it was an act of love. He'd never wanted that from a partner. Never expected it. Hell, he'd ensured no one got close enough to even risk falling in love with him before Calla.

But holding the warm mug between his fingers, he desperately wanted to hear her say it was love. Because it was for him. Calla was his other half…a simple truth that carried so much with it.

Maybe it was cowardly to want her to say it first. To want her to admit he was hers before he announced that truth, too, but Kostas felt like the world tilted as he waited for her to finish the sentence.

"An act of kindness." She laughed, but it was her nervous one.

He kissed her cheek, enjoying the intimate moment. He wanted to scream that he loved her, that he wanted millions more moments like this. But she'd hesitated and the last thing he wanted was to push her. "Thank you for the coffee."

She looked at the mug in his hand then at him. "I haven't had anything but decaf since I found out I was expecting. You don't know how much I wanted to pour myself a cup, too."

He took a sip of the coffee and sighed as the hot liquid hit his tongue. Rationally, he knew the caffeine took at least ten minutes to start showing effect, but the placebo effect was real.

"You can safely have one cup a day." Pregnant mothers were advised to limit their caffeine intake, but didn't have to resist it completely. It was a valid statement, but not the words he wanted to utter.

"If I have one, I will crave more." She looked at his cup once more as she sat next to him on the bed.

He slipped his arm around her waist, his heart calming as she settled in his embrace. He could stay like this forever, but unfortunately, duty called.

Lifting the mug, he took one more sip of coffee before broaching the topic. "So, how well do you know your neighbors?"

"Do you mean how well do I know their schedules, or do I know them enough that they might keep a secret if they see you?"

He hated the defensive tone in her voice. It was

fair. This was not a conversation he wanted to have, either. Mentally, he kicked himself for not getting up when his alarm had gone off hours ago.

"Both, unfortunately." He rubbed her side as he kissed her cheek.

"Unfortunately, the answer is the same for both questions. I've never monitored the schedules of Patrick and his boys. They're teenagers. They go to school, and I think have jobs, but I don't know where or what time. Isabella and Pietro are usually leaving for work at the same time I do, but I don't know their weekend schedules."

Her voice trailed off for a moment then she started again. "As far as keeping secrets, we are on first-name, wave-and-say-hello-neighbor level. Not best friends and confidants. Certainly not 'don't sell the biggest story the island has seen since the birth of its princess to the press.'"

Their news was bigger than the birth of Zelia. The princess was exciting, but she'd been expected, and the second in line to the throne. A pregnant foreigner, an out-of-wedlock baby by the Prodigal Prince, was a bigger story. One he doubted anyone besides Ioannis and Eleni could be trusted with.

He tightened his arm around her and kissed her head. "I'm pretty good at sneaking out of places." He rushed on at the sight of her raised eyebrow. "I mean that I have spent most of my life leaving shops, restaurants and clubs through side and back entrances. Head down, ball cap on. You know, pro-celebrity stuff."

Calla grinned, and he enjoyed the light moment. "I can't think of you as a celebrity. I mean… I know you're a prince. But to me you're just Kostas. My Kostas."

He set his coffee cup on the nightstand then pulled her into his lap. "That is my favorite thing to be."

Maybe that was why their connection had felt so natural. When they'd met, he'd kept his royal status under wraps, and when she'd learned of it, it wasn't the thing she'd cared most about. Rather, it was how he was with her, how their interactions were.

If he didn't have a title, Calla would treat him the same way she did now. It was the best gift; one she likely didn't even register she was giving him.

"You could always spend the day with me. Hunker down here until it's late again." She winked, and he knew it was a serious offer. "I have enough leftovers to last us until tomorrow morning. I will even let you make a second pot of coffee tomorrow before work."

"That sounds like heaven." It was an offer he wished he could take. But Sunday was the day of the week that Ioannis set aside to have all the royals together. Something she'd have to join soon.

It gave them a chance to run over news, any issues that needed to be addressed for the country,
and weekly appearances. Eleni was on maternity
leave and Kostas's work at the clinic kept him
busy, so it was really on Ioannis making appearances. But they discussed it every week. Even if
there was nothing for him or Eleni to do, Ioannis expected everyone there.

No. His brother *wanted* everyone there. Wanted
them to participate. His father had demanded
their presence. Ioannis was different, but that
didn't change the obligation that came with Kostas's birth. The obligation that their child would
have one day too.

She brushed her lips against his. "I understand.
But you should head out. The longer you are here,
the later it gets, the more likely..." Calla swallowed.

He didn't need her to complete the sentence. "I
will see you first thing tomorrow morning at the
clinic. We can video chat this evening?"

She nodded and smiled, but it didn't quite
reach her eyes.

"We could go public?" The phrase was out before he'd thought it through. But he wouldn't pull
it back. He was ready to announce to the world
that Calla was pregnant, that they were getting
married. Ready for the world to see her by his
side each day.

Calla patted his knee, kissed his cheek, and

stood. "I'd like to make that decision based on how we feel. Not for a moment of us oversleeping and trying to game reactions."

"Fair," Kostas said, hoping the disappointment he felt wasn't apparent on his face. He wanted to decide based on feelings, too…and he was already comfortable. But he wouldn't push her.

Unless she and our child are caught in the press's crossfire.

Then he'd do anything he had to, to protect them.

She tightened the belt of her robe and left as he gathered his clothes.

Calla was standing by the door, holding a travel mug, when he exited her room. "Figured you might as well take the rest of it with you."

He took the coffee from her hand. "Thank you. I will see you tonight, on video chat. If you need anything…" He dipped his mouth to hers.

Her hand grazed his cheek as she deepened the kiss. It felt possessive, and he loved every second.

When she broke away, Calla's lips parted as she wrapped her arms around herself. "A kiss just to remind you of me through the day." Her cheeks colored as she looked at him. "It's a silly thing my parents always did…"

"I like that tradition!" Kostas dropped a light kiss to her lips; uncertain he'd ever make it out the door if he kissed her like that again. "We are definitely keeping that one!"

He opened her door, took a quick look. "The coast looks clear." Kostas turned once more and kissed her.

"'Bye, Kostas."

He grinned, loving the look of contentment on her face.

"Prince Kostas?" His name sent a chill down his spine as he turned to find a young man standing at the edge of the hallway, sliding his phone into his back pocket.

"Close the door, Calla." He didn't wait to make sure she did as he asked as he started toward the teen. He shifted his shoulders, donning the mask of Prince Kostas that he dropped so effectively around Calla.

"I'm checking on one of the midwives from the clinic. We had a long delivery yesterday." He hated the lie, but to protect Calla and the baby, he'd do anything necessary.

"By kissing her?" The boy raised an eyebrow, his face shifting as Kostas failed to react. With any luck, the teen was wondering if the story was worth pressing. "Calla is nice."

"She is," Kostas confirmed. *Please let that be enough to keep your mouth shut.* He wanted Calla to choose him, to choose the life they'd have together as Kostas and Calla. But that life would mean they'd also be prince and princess.

Making sure the young man was looking at him, Kostas kept his tone regal, hoping it might gain him something for once in his life. "It would be a shame if anything hurt her."

The teen looked over Kostas's shoulder, and Kostas looked back with him. Calla had shut her door. The boy frowned. Clearly hoping he might catch another glimpse, something to add to his tale.

"It would." He pulled keys from his pocket.

"She doesn't deserve that." Kostas pressed, hoping he was making it clear.

"Have a nice day, Prince Kostas." Then the young man unlocked his apartment and stepped inside without looking back.

Kostas's heart raced as he stared at the closed door then back at Calla's.

Is he going to say anything? Had he snapped a picture?

His phone dinged, and it didn't surprise him to see Calla's text.

Did Nico say anything? Patrick's car isn't in the parking lot, but I can talk to him later.

A few seconds later, a second came.

If you think it will help?

He stared at the messages for a minute, not knowing what to say. Nico seemed to agree that hurting Calla was wrong. That she didn't deserve it. With luck, he'd not gotten a picture and would keep the information to himself. Maybe just this once.

Leave it be for now. If the story breaks, we'll handle it.

He hit Send, then added,

Together. We'll handle it together.

Midwife Tempting Prince!

The headline didn't surprise her. Nico seemed like a good kid, but he had juicy gossip. Keeping that news secret would have been a miracle. Still, it wasn't the way she'd wanted the world to find out about their relationship.

Kostas was right. They should have gone public, beaten the story to the press. But she hadn't wanted him to feel trapped. So much of their relationship seemed to be outside their control.

She was pregnant. They enjoyed each other's company. Calla sighed as she pulled her hair into a bun. It was more than that.

She'd almost called making the coffee yesterday an act of love. Maybe a silly label for what so many would think of as a minor thing. But she hadn't regretted him oversleeping. She'd loved that he'd stayed the whole night.

Loved sleeping next to him. Loved him…

There was one positive to the article. It omitted the rebel or the Prodigal Prince narrative Kostas hated. In fact, based on the reading, it seemed like she was a siren who'd trapped a paragon of virtue. What would the island think when they learned she was pregnant?

She swallowed as she opened her makeup drawer. That was a problem for another day. Today she wanted to walk out of her apartment and confidently into the clinic. She twisted open the tube of mascara, glaring at it.

Calla rarely wore much makeup to the clinic. But the other thing the internet-hit piece had pointed out was her blue robe. They'd called it well-used and sad-looking.

Not good enough for a prince.

Those words hadn't made it into print, but everyone could read between the lines. Her eyes twitched to the robe hanging on the back of the bathroom door.

It was faded and she'd restitched the hem several times. Liam had hated the robe. In fact, he'd gifted her several over the course of their relationship. All frilly things that provided little to no coverage.

But her blue robe was comfortable. Her mother had wrapped it for the last Christmas they'd spent together. Maybe it wasn't fancy, but she'd liked it. It was more faded now, but still just as comfy as it had been on day one. And Kostas hadn't seemed to mind it yesterday.

She'd seen him eye the robe. Or, more accurately, the loose tie around her waist that showed off her cleavage. Yesterday morning had been so perfect.

And now everyone knew.

Calla squared her shoulders and looked at herself in the mirror. She let her hand rest over her belly for a moment as she raised her chin. She was about to walk the first of what she expected would be many gauntlets.

A smile twitched at the corners of her lips, and she gave in to it. Their relationship didn't embarrass her. Maybe it wasn't the perfect way for the world to find out. However, she would not hide herself away as though she'd done something wrong.

"And you'll have everything brought here while we're at the clinic? Just bring everything but the bed and kitchen table and chairs. Not sure what is hers, but we can send back anything that isn't tomorrow. I want all this done while we're at the clinic."

Natalia nodded and made notes on the tablet that seemed permanently affixed to her. "I'll see which room is free for the furniture." She made another note then turned to start her day.

"Room? Furniture?"

Kostas turned and smiled at his brother. "Yes. I'm moving Calla into the palace today. I told you I was pretty sure one of her neighbors snapped a picture of us. Well, they did and sold it…apparently."

Ioannis held up his hands. "Yes. That is unfortunate. I like Calla a lot. She was lovely when helping Eleni, and I know you are drawn to her."

Kostas crossed his arms, visions of his father blinking in the forefront of his memory. "But?" He was proud that his voice sounded calm.

"But moving her into the palace will give the impression that this is serious. Are you ready to take that step? Is Calla?" Eleni stepped to her husband's side and nodded, confirming that she'd read her husband's thoughts perfectly.

Would he and Calla be able to do that someday? Speak with nearly one mind?

"Is there anything I need to pick up for Calla or the baby?"

Natalia's question hit his back as he watched his sister-in-law's eyes widen. Without looking at his assistant, Kostas muttered, "Just make sure the kitchen has decaf coffee."

"And ensure no one interrupts us for a while," Ioannis added.

Kostas pushed a hand through his hair as he

looked at his brother. He'd wanted to tell Ioannis and Eleni with Calla present. Wanted to announce the wedding and the baby with fanfare.

That moment was gone, but he still smiled as he looked from his brother to Eleni. "Yes. Calla is pregnant. Due in a little more than seven months."

"Congratulations. But you should have told us." Ioannis rubbed his face as he looked at him.

Kostas knew this was a lot, but he tried to make Ioannis understand. "We found out the night Zelia was born. We didn't want to steal the spotlight, and Calla wanted us to date. To make sure we were right for each other."

"Are you sure?" Eleni's question hung in the quiet hall.

Three simple words with the simplest answer. "Yes." He nodded. "I never expected this, but yes. I am certain. And I need her moved into the palace, Ioannis. Need her protected."

"Of course. We'll make sure it happens."

His phone buzzed and he took a deep breath as he saw the clinic number pop up and answered, "Dr. Drakos."

"Kali and I showed up early. There are a lot of cameras here. Even more than when the queen gave birth." Alexa sounded breathless as she called out, "No comment and stay out of the clinic. Only patients and staff!"

"Is Calla there yet?" Kostas's stomach flipped. He'd thought he had a little longer.

"No. But Kali is standing by the entrance, looking for her. We've called all the morning appoints for anyone low risk and less than thirty weeks and rescheduled."

"Good call. I'm on my way."

Calla didn't have a car. She walked the few blocks from her apartment to the clinic. If he hurried, he might make it to her place before she headed out. If the clinic was packed, he could only imagine what her apartment complex looked like.

He looked at Ioannis, but his brother waved him off.

"Go. I understand." He wrapped his arm around Eleni and kissed her cheek.

The trip to Calla's apartment felt like it took hours. He tapped his fingers on the steering wheel of his car, trying to avoid the urge to put the pedal to the floor. The parking lot was busting at the seams. He didn't even attempt to pull into the lot. Instead, he parked on a side street and walked with purpose past the comments and questions. His royal mask firmly in place.

"Calla!" He knocked on her door. "Calla." A few flashbulbs went off, but he didn't look at them.

"Good morning, Kostas." She beamed as she

reached for his hand. "Quite a way to start a morning!"

"You seem to be handling it better than expected." Kostas whispered as he squeezed her hand, well aware of the phones and cameras snapping around them.

Calla nodded. "Getting angry or upset doesn't change the facts. Besides, I'm not embarrassed to be with you. Though maybe I need a new robe."

Kostas dropped her hand and put his arm around her waist. It shielded her and the baby a little more. He'd hated the comment about the robe. Or rather, the knowledge that a stupid line in an online tabloid piece had caused it. "I like your robe."

"You're the only one," Calla muttered.

"Not true. You like it." Kostas squeezed her tightly. Her world had altered as of this morning. And it would continue to do so, but she needed to hold on to the little things. To know that she could like a comfy robe and anything else she had.

She was good enough for him just as she was… now he just had to protect her from as much of the royal world as he could!

CHAPTER TEN

THE INSIDE OF the clinic was nearly silent. Most of the noise came from the low hum of the multitude gathered outside. Clicks of cameras and shouted questions, like the door would magically open and she or Kostas would step outside.

Calla wished there was something to do…anything to take her mind off the bizarre situation taking place around her. Kostas was taking the unexpected break in patients to complete paperwork he'd let pile up. Alexa was spinning in the chair typically reserved for the office assistant they'd sent home over an hour ago. And Calla was doing her best not to pace the small room or peek out the window.

She'd offered to head back to her apartment, but Kostas had vetoed that idea with gusto. He'd pointed out that dividing the journalists, photographers and curiosity seekers wouldn't serve until the palace had security in place for her.

Security… She still couldn't wrap her head around that.

When Calla pointed out that Kostas went where he wanted, Alexa had unhelpfully reminded her that Kostas wasn't as interesting as the foreign midwife he'd fallen for. Before she could utter a word, Kostas had agreed. Then he'd stated that he had a security detail that just did little more than hang outside in the parking lot and accompany him to events.

The two men who looked like they stepped out of a movie script were currently guarding the door of the clinic. Georgios and Christos…even their names sounded like characters. But they'd managed to control the crowd outside. *Mostly.*

The phone rang and Alexa picked it up before the second ring. The person on the other line didn't have enough time to utter more than two words before Alexa stated, "No comment," and slammed the receiver down.

"Sorry." Calla frowned, wondering how many times the phone could withstand that level of damage. "I can answer the phone…"

"And deal with rude questions?" Alexa shook her head. "Nope. I slammed that too hard, must admit, I've always wanted to slam a phone down in disgust, but never really had a good excuse. My husband says I'm his overdramatic queen!"

"No. Overdramatic?" Calla playfully tossed her hand to the side and winked at Alexa. "How could he say that?"

Alexa grinned then the giggles escaped her

lips. "I know, right! It's like he knows me far too well."

Calla enjoyed the few moments of levity until the phone rang again. She glared at it and braced herself for the slam as Alexa lifted it again.

"How far apart are the contractions?"

Calla's ears perked. A call not related to her dating life was a welcome respite.

"Three minutes. They came on fast. No, it's okay, Dimitra. That's normal, but we need to see you as soon as possible."

Calla's heart picked up at the mom's name. Dimitra was one of their oldest patients. She and her husband had tried for years to conceive and had never expected a pregnancy just before she turned forty-three.

Dimitra's pregnancy was textbook. There'd been no complications at all, but the woman was understandably anxious. She came to each appointment with a list of questions, having read every prenatal and postnatal book Calla had heard of, and several she hadn't.

In a normal situation, Dimitra would be nervous, and the situation at the clinic was anything but normal.

"And you're trying to get through the gaggle of people out front, but they won't let you in…"

Calla saw red. A patient—her patient—was in labor, and no one was letting her into the clinic. That would not do!

"Calla! No!"

She heard Alexa's plea as she raced for the clinic door. Flashbulbs and questions blended together as she stepped into the chaos.

"Princess!" A hand reached for her, and she blinked as one of Kostas's bodyguards gripped her arm.

"I'm not a princess." She called over the slew of questions being hurled at her.

Christos raised a brow as if to say, *Not yet*, but wisely held his tongue.

"Princess? Does that mean you and Kostas are getting married?"

"How long have you known each other?"

"Did you know each other in Seattle?"

The questions floated around her, but Calla pushed them away.

Where was Dimitra? She scanned the gathered crowd, blinking as flashes went off all around her.

"Ugh." Calla tried to push past the horde, but it seemed to morph together as she moved forward.

"I have a pregnant mom in labor at the back of this crowd. They won't let her through. Help me."

Georgios nodded and gestured to his partner. With no trouble, they created a small path through the mess.

Ignoring the questions, Calla called out for Dimitra as she walked with the bodyguards. Rising on her tiptoes, she wished for the millionth time in her life that she had more height.

"There's a hand raised to the left. Looks to be a heavily pregnant woman. Stay here, Princess."

"Not a princess!" Calla huffed but agreed. She'd argue with the Christos over titles another time.

Georgios stepped to her side but didn't say anything as he glared at the gathered crowd.

Christos was back in moments but without Dimitra. "She's breathing really hard and can't fully stand."

"Get me to her now!"

She delivered the order, and the two men seemed to part the people before her as if by magic.

Dimitra was leaning over her knees. Her face flushed. "I feel like I need to push." Her eyes were wide as she looked at Calla. Her bottom lip wobbled. "It's happening so fast. Leo dropped me off. He is back there. He can't miss this. He can't." Her sobs hiccupped as another contraction started.

Calla turned to look at the clinic door. It was a little over two hundred meters. A distance that shouldn't take more than a minute or so to walk…assuming you weren't in active labor. She looked over Dimitra's shoulder and saw Leo farther back in the group, desperately trying to push his way toward his wife.

"Dimitra." Calla waited for her to look up then she kept her voice level. "We will not have a baby in the parking lot. I promise."

Turning to the bodyguard to her left, she pointed to the clinic. Kostas was by the entrance, or at least she thought he was, based on the shift in the questions around her. "I need a wheelchair, Christos." He looked at the clinic, but she grabbed his arm. "And Kostas needs to get washed up. Tell him that has to be his focus. I am fine, but Dimitra needs to push. We may deliver in the lobby. Tell him that!"

The man looked at Dimitra and then nodded. "Of course."

Turning her attention to the other bodyguard, Calla pointed to Leo. "Georgios! Get that man and bring him here."

"I'm not leaving you, Princess."

She understood his job, but now was not the time. She was not a princess...at least not yet. And even after she gained a title, her patients would still come first. The sooner everyone understood that, the better.

Calla grabbed his arm and turned him toward Leo. "I am not asking! That man *will* see the birth of his first child. Go get him. That's an order." If he was going to call her "princess," she may as well act like one at the moment!

The man waffled; she could see the look in Georgios's eyes as he weighed the situation before him. She understood what she was asking, but Leo deserved to be here with his wife.

"Please."

Dimitra's plea broke his final resolve and he darted off.

"I know this isn't the way you planned for delivery." Calla kept her voice down, trying to pretend that there weren't dozens of ears around them listening in.

"With a soon-to-be princess?" Dimitra chuckled then bent over again.

She knew it was nerves and trying not to focus on her own predicament that made Dimitra laugh. Heaven knew Calla had laughed in more than one situation where it wasn't technically appropriate.

"That's what they say." Calla smiled, hoping it looked real as she focused on her patient.

"I need to push!"

"Not now." Calla tapped Dimitra's shoulder, firming up her voice. "I know it's hard. Look at me."

She saw a few eyes widen at her tone, but sometimes health professionals had to use strict voices to get their patient's attention. And if ever a situation called for it!

Holding up a finger, she bit her lip and wished the wheelchair was already there. "Pretend this is a candle and blow it out."

It was a trick her midwife mentor had taught

her. The action helped mothers stop pushing, but it wouldn't stop it forever. The crush of people around her had stopped hurling questions, but she knew people were filming, taking pictures of what should be a private experience.

She would not let Dimitra deliver here. They might only get to the front of the clinic, but she deserved more privacy than this.

"Dimitra!" Leo's voice was tight as he came to his wife's side.

"Look at me," Calla ordered. She was glad Leo was there, but Dimitra and her baby were her top priority. "Blow."

"Princess!"

Seriously, was there nothing else Christos would call her? But he had a wheelchair, so she let it go…again.

They loaded Dimitra into the chair and raced for the clinic entrance.

"We're in room one!" Alexa called out.

"I need to push! I can't… I can't…dear God, Calla, there is so much pressure."

"Kostas!"

He exited the room, his eyes scanning her briefly as he took in the scene.

"I think the baby is crowning." She couldn't be sure, but based on the need Dimitra was feeling, it was likely.

Kostas bent, raising the hem of Dimitra's dress. "Calla's right. We aren't even going to make it to the room. Leo, put your hands under Dimitra's arms to give her a little help."

Dimitra took a deep breath and bore down as the next contraction took over. It took only two pushes before Kostas grinned and held up their very loud little man.

"Congratulations." Calla felt her lips tip up as Kostas laid the little one in Dimitra's arms without even detaching the cord. He then nodded to Alexa to slowly wheel the new family back to room one so they could fully take care of their patients.

"So what now?" Calla sat on the desk and dropped a kiss on Kostas's lips, then yawned as she looked at the clock. Kali had arrived about ten minutes ago. She'd watch over Dimitra and her little man until they were ready to be discharged. Calla wasn't looking forward to braving the group outside again, but she also did not want to sleep at the clinic.

Kostas stood and pulled her into his arms. He dropped a kiss on the top of her head as he squeezed her tightly. "We go home."

"Home?" Calla looked at him. "You're going to spend the night at my place again? I mean, you're more than welcome, of course." She sighed. Sleeping next to Kostas, waking up next to him, had been perfect. Even if the repercussions were sitting outside.

"The palace, Calla. Home."

She blinked. The palace... She knew that they'd end up there eventually. Their child was a prince or princess; their father was third in line to the throne. But she had a hard time thinking of it as home.

Though if she was honest, the small apartment hadn't felt like home, either...until Kostas spent the night.

He was her home. And if that meant the palace, so be it.

"I need to get a few things."

"I had all of your things sent to the palace while we were here." Kostas released his hold on her as she stepped back.

The room spun as she tried to place those words. "So when I offered to go back to the apartment today?" She gripped her waist as she looked at the man in front of her. The one she loved, who'd moved her things...without asking. Without even telling her!

"They were moving your belongings. Yes." Kostas's voice was firm. The prince delivering the news.

She chuckled, but there was no mirth in the sound. The last twelve hours had been over the top, but there was no way the palace knew what to take and what to leave in her apartment. "And how did Natalia know what to move? I seem to remember refusing that overture two weeks ago!"

"They moved the entire apartment." Kostas sighed. "I know this is a lot—"

She held up her hand, cutting him off. "The entire apartment? The furniture is rented, as is the cutlery...and..." Calla blew out a breath and moved to the chair, flopping down.

This was fine. Everything was fine. It was.

Kostas went to the floor in front of her. Even sitting on his knees, his dark eyes were nearly at eye level with hers. "I know this a lot. But I will do everything to keep you and the baby safe. And you are safest with me at the palace, Calla."

Given the pressure of the press outside, she nodded. He got a pass. This time. But she wanted to be sure he understood her position...now. "Next time, you will tell me. If we are going to do this, we do it together. As a team. Understood."

"A team." He kissed her cheek. "I like the sound of that. A lot."

"Good." Calla nodded, her breaths coming a little easier.

He put his hands on her knees, his fingers running over them before he pushed a lock of hair that had slipped from her bun back behind her ear. "I have something else for you."

"A ring?" Calla groaned but cut the sound off as she saw the reflection of the truth in his eyes. "Kostas..."

"I know you wanted more time, Calla. But..."

He flipped open the box. The shimmering diamond was massive and surrounded by smaller emeralds. "Over the top" was the best description. It was beautiful, but the exact opposite of what she'd have chosen for herself.

The ring was a thing made for a royal. Something her child would be. But she...

Calla's parents had loved each other, but they'd been lower middle class when the restaurant was doing well. When it wasn't...well, then they'd had to decide which bills were most important.

How many times had Liam's parents stated she wasn't good enough for their son?

And now she was sitting across from a real prince. A real Cinderella story. But Cinderella and her Prince Charming had loved each other. She loved Kostas, but this ring was not a declaration of love. It was protection.

A statement for others, not for her.

Her heart screamed for her to say yes. It yearned for Kostas, for happily ever after. Her brain urged caution.

"Calla?"

She looked up from the ring, meeting Kostas's eyes. "That is a lot for a ring."

Kostas moved the box, so it sparkled in the light. "It makes a statement."

She ran her hand along his cheek, working up the courage to ask the question she needed answered most.

"Are you sure?"

The words sounded wrong.

Because they are…

She should have asked *Do you love me?* That was the question she wanted answered. The one that was so important but sounded so needy.

Kostas wasn't Liam, yet the desire to be her own person, to show that she wasn't the needy girl, the one who'd stand in front of someone and ask if they loved them, was overwhelming.

A grin spread across his face until Kostas looked like he was beaming. "I'm certain!"

She let go of as many worries as possible as she let his certainty flow through her. Holding out her finger, she tried not to let her mouth gape as he slid the rock on her hand. She was engaged…to a prince.

No.

She was engaged to Kostas. And that was better than any fantasy.

"Are you ready? The second we step out the door with that ring on your finger, the entire island will know that we're engaged."

Clasping her hand in his, Calla took a deep breath.

"Ready."

CHAPTER ELEVEN

"Good morning, Princess."

Kostas's words wrapped around her as she rolled over in the massive bed. *Their massive bed.* He'd slept better than he had in forever. Having Calla next to him was the best feeling in the world.

"I'm not a princess, at least not yet. No matter what Christos and Georgios said yesterday."

Running his hand down her side, he kissed her. It wasn't much of a kiss. Not passionate, but it felt special. The world looked for passion, for the big moments, but it was these little ones that made for a happy life.

Now that he'd found it, he'd do anything to protect it. To protect her and their child.

"It's a term associated with royal fiancées in Palaío too. You aren't Your Royal Highness until after we wed, but you became a princess when we got engaged. The best way to protect the baby and you."

"So you told the staff we were engaged before you asked me?" Calla blinked. "What if I'd said no?"

Kostas held up her hand, enjoying the sight of the large ring on her finger. No one would doubt that he cared for her if they saw this. The ring screamed *princess*.

But his stomach pinched at the tone in her voice. "Calla, I assumed you didn't want to announce the pregnancy, at least not yet. Though we won't be able to keep it quiet much longer."

"Meaning?" She sat up, pulling the covers with her.

He moved with her, trying to find the right words. "I can't give palace protection to my girlfriend. Ioannis is not my father, but a full-time staff and security, who you'll meet shortly, is not possible unless we announced your pregnancy or our engagement."

"So this way we protect my privacy and the baby." Calla swallowed. There was an underlying thread to her statement, but he couldn't quite understand what it might be.

"I will keep you two safe. I promise."

"Safe? What—"

A knock at the door interrupted whatever she was about to say. It was lost as Natalia and Angeliki entered. "Good morning. Sorry to interrupt, but there are a few things we should get ahead of before the event tonight."

"Event?" Calla rolled off the bed and grabbed

her blue robe, covering her tank top and short shorts. Putting on her glasses, she pushed her hair out of her face.

"The king and queen are holding a small reception to properly announce your engagement."

He understood why Calla was focused on the word *event*, but it was the beginning of the statement that sent chills down his spine. "What 'things'?"

He saw Natalia's gaze shift to Angeliki. The woman was Calla's assistant, and the fact that she adjusted her shoulders as she met Kostas's and Calla's looks confirmed his suspicions. "What does the news say this morning?"

"They are saying the princess was rude to a bodyguard and a pregnant woman yesterday. That she is already giving orders and acting like a diva. And that she will ruin you. The language is less flattering than that."

Kostas sucked in a deep breath. None of that was fair. Eleni was the loved one, and they'd cast Calla in the opposite role. The truth failing to matter.

Calla laughed. The sound echoing off the walls of the room. The women seemed as stunned as he was at seeing his soon-to-be bride's mirth at the situation. She clapped and walked to the closet.

"Look at that, Kostas. We've rehabilitated your image." She winked as she opened the door. "You just had to fall for a diva. I've had a few rows with patients, but even in the throes of labor pains, no one has ever called me a diva."

"This isn't funny, sweetheart. If they are making such statements, it means they are making you the villain. The roles they choose in the first few weeks will stick." Kostas kept his voice even though he wanted to dictate a forceful response and demand its immediate publication through their social media.

"If you're the villain, then so is our child." He pushed again. "We have to respond."

"No. We don't." Calla kissed his cheek as she emerged from the closet with a pair of worn blue jeans and T-shirt. "Do you see me as the villain?"

"Of course not." Kostas felt his head pop back at the ridiculous question.

"Do either of you?" Calla asked the assistants, who both shook their heads no. "Do you think Alexa or Kali will think me the villain, or Ioannis or Eleni?"

"No," Kostas muttered. "But that doesn't mean that we just let this stand. We need to make sure they see us as above this. Know that we won't stand for lies."

"Kostas, you can't fight every battle."

"For our child—" *for you* "—I certainly can."

He hated the exasperation he saw dripping from Calla, but she needed to understand. Ignoring the mistruths didn't make them go away.

His mother and Maria hadn't had someone to respond for them. Calla would...always.

"Fine. If you want to issue a rebuttal, go for it. But I doubt it fixes anything." Calla held up her jeans then looked at the assistants.

"I hate to be a diva they're accusing me of being on day one, but any chance Eleni has some belly bands? You know, the stretchy bands most women wear early when their pants get a little snug? I should have thought to order some, but everything's been..." Calla blew out a breath as she forced a smile. "Would hate for the press to get a picture of my unbuttoned pants and jump to any conclusions. Even if they were right, this time."

Her tone was playful, but he could hear a hint of fear. She was putting on a brave face, but Calla was nervous. That, he understood.

"We'll find something, and we have a few dresses, too, for tonight's party for you to choose from. Nothing in your closet works for the function," Angeliki stated as she made a few notes on the tablet identical to the one Natalia carried around.

Kostas saw Calla blink and he reached for her hand. "Angeliki meant that, for a royal function, we need formal wear, and you understandably didn't bring that with you."

"Of course." Calla offered him a tight smile. "Not a lot of room in my bag for long gowns."

He squeezed her hand before turning back to the assistants. "I'll work on the reply for the media, run it through the press secretary, and I need to swing by the clinic and check on Dimitra."

"I'll come too." Calla brightened.

Before he could say anything, Angeliki rushed in. "We have some things we need to get set up here, Princess. It's your day off, correct?" She looked from the tablet to Calla to Kostas.

"It is." She hesitated and Kostas pulled her to him.

She softened in his arms and leaned her head against his chest. "I know this is a lot, sweetheart." He squeezed her tightly. "But we'll be fine. Promise."

"We're a team, remember."

"We are." Kostas nodded. But team or not, he would not allow the public to make the woman he loved a villain. She would not suffer the way his mother had. He'd protect her at all costs.

Kissing her again, he let her go. "I can't wait to see the dress you pick out for tonight. You'll be perfect. Everyone will think so."

Calla rolled her eyes. "I'm not trying to be perfect, Kostas." She kissed his cheek then let Angeliki direct her to the door.

"Champagne or hors d'oeuvres, Princess?"

Calla waved away the waiter for what felt like

the hundredth time. The room was full of people snacking and drinking. She couldn't consume any alcohol and the small trays of food turned her stomach.

So far, she'd rarely had issues with morning sickness, but her stomach was tossing too much at the moment to put anything in it.

"How are you holding up?" Eleni's voice was quiet and only for her ears as Calla stood in the crowded room.

In theory, this was the party celebrating her and Kostas's impending nuptials, but she'd chosen nothing. No input on the flowers, the food, drinks, the messaging. Even her dress was the only one from Eleni's closet that had fit her petite frame. It was not how she'd imagined an engagement party. Though, she'd never anticipated marrying royalty. Perhaps this was just the way it was.

Pursing her lips, she resisted the urge to shrug, knowing tons of eyes were trained on all her movements.

"Overwhelming." Calla offered Eleni what she hoped was close to a cheerful smile to cover the unsettledness tugging at her back.

Eleni slid her hand through Calla's as they started toward another area of the party, casually making conversation with a few people as they walked past. Eleni was an expert at making others feel comfortable without actually saying anything too deep. It was a skill Calla had seen Kostas use too. But it felt wrong.

At least for her.

She understood the need to guard herself. But she wanted to be genuine. There would be days where she was happy, others where she was cross. She didn't want to wear a royal mask. She wanted the people of Palaío to see her exactly as she was.

A midwife, a soon-to-be mom, a wife who loved her husband...even if they fought occasionally. She wasn't interested in the fairy tale. She wanted the real thing.

Kostas found her across the crowd, saw she was with Eleni, and nodded. She'd had no time alone since she'd been in her apartment putting on makeup to prepare for the rabid press outside her door. How had that only been a day ago?

"He's talking to one of the television anchors..."

"No doubt reiterating the palace's line regarding me. Trying to make me seem perfect." Calla bit the inside of her cheek as the words left her lips. "Sorry, Eleni."

"Don't be." The queen hugged her. "This is a lot, Calla." She paused, checked their location, and then motioned for Calla to follow her.

They stepped into a small room, and Eleni squeezed her hands. "Are you sure about this?"

Calla hesitated. She wanted to say yes. She was sure about Kostas. It was the prince she wavered on. He claimed they were one and the same, but they weren't. The mask he wore around others, the buttoned-up man trying so hard to prove that he wasn't the rebellious teen, was hard to watch.

He deserved to be who he was, the kind-hearted, playful man who enjoyed silly coffee mugs and had come home to ensure the people of his island had access to a great OBGYN. He cared what they thought of him...and what they thought of her.

What if the press never changed its thoughts on her? Calla didn't mind, as long as Kostas didn't treat her differently. But could he separate the two? She didn't need protection from poisoned pens—at least, not all the time. She just wanted his love.

"I don't know." It was honest, but she saw Eleni's eyes dip. Calla hated disappointing her, but she would not pretend things were fine if they weren't. She'd sworn not to do that again after her last relationship. It was hard, but she'd stand in her own truth. Even if it wasn't what others wanted to hear.

"I lo—" She caught herself, though she suspected Eleni knew she'd been about to say she loved Kostas. He deserved to hear that first.

"A marriage of convenience..." she continued,

"well, it's just not the way I envisioned things." Her stomach rumbled and she laughed. "Guess I should have eaten something."

"That is easily rectified." Eleni grinned, but it didn't quite meet her eyes. She reached for the door handle then paused.

"Calla…" She sighed as she seemed to weigh her words. "Life is too short not to be certain of your place. I think you are, but Kostas ran away rather than force the island to accept who he truly is. He came home because Ioannis asked him, though I suspect Kostas saw it as an order. He's seeking outside approval, and he may never get it. I don't have an answer for any of that, but wanted you to know."

"I do." Calla nodded. She knew who she was, what she would accept; now she had to hope Kostas would accept that person, as well. And maybe step into his true self full-time too.

"There you are." Kostas beamed as she and Eleni stepped from the room. "I thought maybe you were hiding. This is a lot."

"Do you want to hide?" Calla offered. "We can for a few minutes."

"It's our party, Calla."

"Is it?" She raised a brow.

"Of course." He gestured to the room as Eleni made a silent retreat. "Our names are even on the cake."

"What's the flavor of the cake, Kostas?"

He blinked at her question. "What?"

It was a small thing. But he'd told her yesterday that it mattered that she liked her blue robe. He'd meant it then too. But did he give himself the same grace? The same ability to choose his likes based on what he wanted?

"The flavor of the cake, Kostas. That big, beautiful cake. My favorite flavor is a white cake with raspberry filling, and yours?"

"Dark chocolate with chocolate icing."

"Well, that cake certainly doesn't have chocolate icing. And I suspect there is no raspberry filling." She gestured to the decorations and food. "This is an experience for others, not our party."

Kostas brushed his lips against hers. "I told Natalia and Angeliki to make sure everything was perfect. That no one could find fault with it."

And there was the crux of the problem. He was still terrified of anyone finding fault, or people he didn't know thinking he was the prodigal or rebel prince. "Kostas, people are going to find fault. You—*we* are public figures. You can't stop the tongues wagging. All you can do is find happiness."

With me. Those words felt like too much in the crowded ballroom, but she held them tight within her.

"I am happy." He squeezed her.

She wanted to believe him. But as his eyes

wandered the room, she saw the need for approval, the desire to control the story. She knew he wanted to protect her, but was it really for her?

CHAPTER TWELVE

KOSTAS ROLLED OVER and his hand struck Calla's cool pillow. He sat up, blinking at the sight of the empty place next to him. Rubbing his eyes, he slid off the bed and went looking for Calla.

His stomach twisted as he found the bathroom, dressing room and kitchen empty. The palace was enormous, but Calla had kept to his rooms since moving in a week ago. He sensed she was chafing at the royal life over the last two weeks.

Her life had shifted so quickly. She claimed she was adjusting, but the added attention must be difficult.

She was pushing back on things too. She'd challenged him on the protocols he'd set up for himself after his mother's death and his own fall from grace. The things designed to ensure her safety. He'd tried to compromise. But how could he not respond to the ridiculous story that she'd hated her engagement party and that Eleni had scolded her for being pouty.

He'd wanted to put out a release stating she'd

loved it. She'd told him she wouldn't lie. That if they corrected the story, it needed to be with the truth. That she was finding royal life overwhelming and that the staff had done a lovely job on such short notice. But that she wished she'd had a bit more control over the festivities.

Control.

He understood. The party had been rushed, and the staff had largely put the event together using Eleni and Ioannis's favorite foods and decorations. The flowers were lovely, but Eleni's not Calla's style. The cake was delicious, but Ioannis's favorite lemon rather than his or Calla's.

Yet if they'd put out a statement regarding her wanting control…he could see the twists in real time. So he'd adjusted. Not the full pushback, but not full honesty, either. A carefully worded release that kept the emotion neutral but clarified the lies.

It seemed a new story popped up almost every day…and each day he'd struck back. Correcting the narratives. It was his mission to ensure she was treated as fairly as possible, even if Calla told him it didn't bother her too much.

Maybe it was fine now. But he knew how the stories ripped at you over time. One day it would hurt her, and he never wanted her to doubt that he'd protect her.

He pushed a hand through his hair as he stood in the empty library.

Where could she be?

The clinic? Kostas rushed back to his room. If he'd slept through a notification, surely Calla would have woken him. Except they'd argued about the clinic last night too.

No, "argued" was too strong a word. She'd simply ignored his suggestion about reducing her hours at the clinic. The press wasn't hanging out quite like vultures anymore, but they still cased the clinic more than he'd like. It was the place where she was easiest to find.

He'd already put out feelers for a new midwife. When the baby was born, she'd have to step back a bit. And Dr. Bandi had agreed to Ioannis's terms. She'd just started. Soon Kostas would have a more regular schedule. Handle half the patients rather than all of them!

"The princess is on the beach." Christos yawned as he walked past Kostas. "Antonio is with her, though, keeping his distance."

The beach? So early?

Kostas nodded as he headed out to find Calla.

Her hair waved in the breeze as she looked across the water. She wasn't in the water, but close enough that when the wave came, it rushed over her toes. He paused and stared at her.

She was lovely, true perfection! Calla looked relaxed for the first time since they'd gone public. Looked like herself. He grabbed his phone out of his back pocket and snapped the photo.

Sliding his phone into his pocket, he took a step forward. She turned and he saw her smile fade. That tore at his heart.

"Don't worry, Antonio isn't far away." She took a deep breath before stepping a little closer to the escaping sea.

"Calla, I was just going to ask if I could join you."

She closed her eyes as the tide rolled over her feet again, seemingly lost in the moment. "I'd like that."

Stepping behind her, he wrapped his arms around her waist and rested his head on hers. For a few precious breaths, he let himself go. Just enjoying the moment with Calla, unworried about any of the responsibilities they had.

"This is nice," Calla murmured as she turned in his arms.

"It is." He tightened his grip then lowered his mouth to capture hers.

"I always wanted to live by the beach. To wake up and play by the ocean. It wasn't something my parents could afford, but I still dreamed about it. Now..." She pulled back, walked a little closer to the water, turned and grinned at him.

Then she bent, scooped a bit of water in her palms and tossed it his way. It was chilly but not cold as it splashed onto his shirt.

Kostas couldn't stop the laughter escaping his lips, even if he'd wanted to. "Is that how it's going to be, Princess?" He raced toward her, scooping water in both his hands before dumping it over her head.

She giggled as she kicked up water at him. He turned so the spray hit his back before he shifted quickly to the side.

"Wait!" Calla held up her hand.

"Calling a pause to the game so quick?" He chucked the water from his hands.

"I think the baby moved. I know it's early..." She sucked in a breath and grabbed his hand, laying it over her lower belly. Her stomach rumbled and she let out a laugh... "Oh, pretty sure that was just hunger pangs. Well, we can pretend for a moment, right?"

She closed her eyes, taking in slow, deep breaths.

They weren't feeling the baby, but as he laid his head against hers, he left his hand where their child lay. These few moments were precious, and he wanted to soak them in.

After a few minutes, she kissed his cheek. "I should probably get some breakfast."

"Probably." Kostas wrapped his arm around her waist as they started back toward the palace.

"This morning was delightful. We should make time for this."

"For playing in the ocean?" Kostas hugged her tightly. "I'd be okay with that."

She bumped her hip against his. "You know

what I mean. Time for Calla and Kostas, not the prince and princess." She rose up on her toes and kissed his cheek.

"We are the same people, sweetheart. Kostas and Calla. Prince and Princess." The sooner she understood that the world wouldn't see a difference, the better.

"Are we?" She leaned her head against his shoulder and before he could say anything, she offered, "Want to help me get the sand off in the shower?"

Desire glittered in her eyes, and he let the fresh worry wash away. "I think this may be the best way to start a day!"

Angeliki's text message landed in Calla's phone, and she sighed as she saw the headline for the article. Someone had captured the image of Kostas with his hand over her belly this morning. They must have had a telescopic lens.

Honestly, it was a great photo. One that she'd set on the mantel if it had resulted from a photoshoot.

But it hadn't.

And the note above it was the reason Angeliki had given her the heads-up.

Prince Marrying Midwife
Because of Pregnancy!

It was her worst fear outlined in blocky letters designed to capture a reader's attention. Angeliki and Natalia were already working with the public relations department for a response. She'd given Calla a ten-minute head start to let Kostas know before Natalia sent the text of the response to him. Waiting wasn't an option, even though her feet dragged as she started for the office.

Opening the door, she swallowed as he looked up from the stack of papers on his desk.

"Hi, sweetheart, are you about ready to head home? I know we have the fundraiser for Eleni's charity. I have a few more things to do, but if you'll just give me ten minutes, then I'll be ready."

The fundraiser to help ensure income didn't stop anyone from continuing their education. It was Eleni's passion, and she'd talked to Calla about joining it. But Calla didn't want to give up being a midwife. She'd have to step back some, but if she was going to have a public platform, she wanted it focused on access to prenatal care.

That was a discussion for another day.

"The pregnancy is public knowledge." The statement fell from her lips. There were hundreds of better ways to start this conversation, all of them flooding her brain after she'd spit out the worst option.

"How?" Kostas stood, and she handed him the phone.

The silence stretched for what seemed like forever as he looked at the article.

"It's an excellent picture." Kostas shrugged as he handed it back to her.

"I thought the same thing." Calla blinked, trying to justify the reaction she'd expected with the one she was getting. Was he finally not caring what they said about him? About her? Willing to let it flow...

And did it have to be this headline he was okay with?

"You're okay?" She bit her lip as he slid back into the chair. "Natalia and Angeliki already have a statement ready to go. It should be in your email shortly. They wanted me to tell you first."

Kostas typed a few more things before he powered down the computer. "I mean it's not the way I'd have announced the news, but at least this headline is mostly true."

"It is?" Calla felt her mouth open wide. Hurt bubbled through her as she tried to catch her breath. She loved him. Had upended her life, given up control of so many things, hoping he felt the same way about her.

Was she just a fool?

No. What they had was special. She didn't doubt that. But that didn't mean it was forever love.

How many times had she started to ask that and held back? So many relationship problems could be handled with a simple conversation… but what if you feared the answers?

"So the headline is true?" Her voice wobbled but she refused to break. Not now.

He looked up, and she could see the moment his words' meaning registered. "No." Kostas shook his head. "No."

He pushed a hand through his hair as he stood. "Calla, I am so sorry. I didn't mean that, not really. I… I just meant that of all the headlines, this one is the closest to the truth. Would you have accepted my proposal if you weren't pregnant?"

No. She bit her lip. It was true, but in this moment she couldn't seem to catch the words exiting her mouth. "You didn't ask me to marry you. You just held up a giant ring."

She gripped her side. "What are we doing, Kostas?" Waves sounded in her ears as she tried to regain her footing. This morning, everything seemed so easy. He'd held her and the doubts she'd had since moving into the palace seemed to evaporate.

Now, though. Everything raced toward her.

"We are protecting our baby…" He grimaced. "That wasn't right, either."

"I think it was." Calla blinked away the tears she felt forming.

"Can we go home? We can talk about this there? Away from any prying ears in the clinic."

"So you don't trust our colleagues?"

"I didn't say that."

"You did," she countered.

"Calla, I just meant that, at the palace, we can be ourselves. We can have this row there, get it out. In private."

"A controlled environment…"

"Exactly."

It wasn't the right answer…but he wasn't wrong, either. They'd seen their last patient, but this was still their workplace. She bit her lip as she tried to cool the emotions pouring through her.

"I'm not waiting for you." Calla stated. "I'll meet you at the palace." Before he could argue, she held up a hand. "I need a few minutes to collect myself. I'll be ready for the event tonight and then we will talk."

She left before he could say anything else.

"Calla?" Alexa's voice was soft. "Are you okay?"

She'd heard everything, but her eyes held kindness, not the look of someone savoring juicy gossip.

Rather than lie or put on a royal mask, Calla shook her head no.

Alexa pulled her into a hug, clasping her tightly. "Can I do anything?"

"Distract my security team." Calla let out a harsh sob. She needed a few minutes on her own. But that was too much to ask.

"I can do that."

"I was joking." Calla wiped a tear from her cheek.

"I wasn't." Alexa winked and waved as she headed for the entrance. "Wait two minutes, then use the emergency exit."

She nodded and then followed Alexa's suggestion.

The late-afternoon sun hit her cheeks as she looked at the sky. It was easier to breathe, but that didn't stop the tears from racing down her cheeks. Without thinking, she climbed the secluded walking path that, if she followed it, would lead her all the way to The Grotto. She wouldn't go that far, but it gave her at least a few minutes of solitude.

Finding a sizable rock, she sat and pulled her knees up to her chest, rocking herself as she gave in to all the hurt Kostas's words had caused.

Even if they are true?

That was the part that struck her hardest. He was right. They might have dated without her pregnancy; she wanted to hope so. But she wouldn't be living in the palace now, wouldn't have the giant ring on her left hand, without the baby.

Kostas was right. Their child needed protection, but Calla deserved a husband who wanted her for her too.

Her phone buzzed and it surprised Calla to

see Angeliki's name under the time. An hour had escaped her.

"Is Kostas frantic?"

"You slipped your security detail, Princess. Of course, he is frantic. If anything happens to the baby..."

The baby...

"I don't need a lecture, Angeliki. I am perfectly fine. Not all that far from the clinic, actually."

"Once the new midwife starts, you'll be here more often, then he won't worry so much."

"What?" The birds took flight and Calla flinched as she focused on lowering her voice. "What do you mean 'new midwife'?"

"Well..." She could hear her assistant swallow. "Maybe it's best if Kostas talks to you about the expectations once you're married."

Expectations.

There it was. The changes she'd feared from the moment he'd put the ring on her finger. The control, the desire for her to be someone other than who she was. Who she wanted to be.

But she wasn't the Perfect Princess the press refused to call her, despite Kostas's many official statements. Not that she wanted to be. And none of which had said he loved her or cared about her. Calla closed her eyes as that truth settled in. He'd corrected the facts of the story...but added no feelings.

"Please tell Kostas I need a little more time, but I'll see him after the charity event."

She muttered a goodbye and started for the palace. She hoped Eleni would forgive her, but Calla had other plans for her evening.

Kostas raced toward his room after the charity event. He'd waited for an hour before realizing that Calla would not attend. He'd watched the clock closely to make sure he'd been in attendance long enough. People wouldn't talk much about him leaving.

Swinging open the door, his chest lightened as he saw her sitting on the bed. She was here; she was safe.

"I'm issuing a statement about the headline. I—"

Calla held up a hand. "Did the clinic hire a new midwife?"

Kostas blinked. He'd anticipated the fight about his statement earlier. He'd spent most of the evening wanting to kick his own ass for it. He wasn't marrying Calla because of the baby, but because he loved her. That was what mattered.

He'd not expected this question. His mouth opened then closed as he tried to make his tongue work.

"Did the clinic hire a new midwife? My replacement."

Kostas shuddered as the word *replacement* reverberated around the room. "Replacement isn't the exact right word."

Calla shook her head as she stood.

"Calla, once our child is born, the duties of a royal…"

"Stop!" She shook as she pushed a tear from her cheek. "I'm not just a royal. I'm a daughter. A friend. A woman. And a midwife. I like my job and even if I didn't, I still owe Liam—"

"No." Kostas shook his head. "Natalia found him and let me know how much. I paid it off before we got engaged."

Calla pursed her lips. "'Paid it off before we got engaged.' Of course you did. Can't have the island think you're marrying a gold digger? That's certainly not the right image. Very far from perfection."

"Hey!" Kostas hated his raised voice. That was not how he'd meant this. He'd done it to free her. So it was one less worry.

Sucking in a deep breath, he tried to keep the emotions he rarely let loose in check. "I did it for you. A fresh start."

"And you never wondered what people might say if they found out I was here paying off a loan to my ex. My wealthy ex."

He hesitated. That hadn't crossed his mind… had it?

She walked to the closet and pulled out her beaten-up luggage. "I wanted Kostas. The funny man who plays in the water with me. Watches bad documentaries and laughs at me sitting on a counter. Not the one so scared of making a mistake in public he tries to control everything possible."

God, she'd spent the evening packing.

She'd never planned to stay with him. To find a middle ground.

"We'll find a way to co-parent." Calla sobbed and swallowed. "But I won't live under a microscope, Kostas."

"That's royal life."

"No." Calla shook her head. "It's not the island's microscope I'm leaving. It's yours. I wanted to be on your team…"

"We are a team!" he challenged.

"Sure. You're just the star and get to make all the decisions, right? Make sure the image is correct, right? Make sure no one thinks we make mistakes! Always controlling the narrative. More worried about what *they* think than what *I* want."

The words cut deep. He'd done his best to make sure no one hurt her like his mother and Maria. He understood this world, understood the challenges. He'd been burned by the scandal, watched his mother lose herself, endured Maria's disgrace because of a teenage romance. He was protecting Calla.

She walked past him.

He wanted to say something. But in the end, he stayed, lost for words as the woman he loved walked out.

CHAPTER THIRTEEN

"THE BABY AND I are fine... Please give the rest of the apartment some space... No, it is not true that I am returning to Seattle." That insidious rumor had popped up as soon as she'd left the palace.

There was nothing in Seattle for her. Her parents were gone, and the clinic had filled her position almost as soon as she'd put in her two-week notice. She'd already let the travel nursing agency know she wouldn't be accepting any more assignments. The island of Palaío was her child's place. And she'd find her path here.

Hopefully, one that didn't involve as much of a spotlight after she had the baby. She smiled through the pain as she nodded to the crowd that had gathered after the reports she'd moved back to her apartment had emerged. She swore some of them were camping out at her home.

Home...

The apartment wasn't home. She'd didn't even have all the furniture back. Though Ioannis had ensured the dishes were returned, the living room furniture was in Dr. Bandi's temporary apartment. A delivery was scheduled at the end of the week, but until then, this was just a sparse shell.

Calla hugged her waist as she stood in the empty living room. She'd managed the last three days by keeping one foot in front of the other. And ensuring she only worked during the new doctor's shift.

Kostas hadn't sought her out.

After making sure he knew where she was and that everything was safe for weeks, he'd simply dropped it. She bit the inside of her cheek, but it didn't stop the tears from falling.

She'd meant what she'd said. She didn't want to live under his microscope. Didn't want to be perfect for the cameras. Calla wanted to be herself, wanted that to be enough. But she wished he'd stopped her. Wished he'd said something...

But what was there to say?

Liam had wanted to mold her into the society wife. It hadn't worked. Kostas had wanted her to be the perfect princess. Above any kind of reproach. Never mind that the island wouldn't see her that way...at least not right away.

After a few years, when the baby was older, when she and Kostas were still a happy couple. Maybe then the narrative might change.

The narrative, the one she claimed not to care about, seemed to encompass her now. The questions, the shouts, the sideways glances, the rumors. They took a toll.

One that would have been worth it…if she and Kostas were a real team.

That was the hurt that cut the deepest. That he hadn't talked to her. Told her the game plan. He'd acted like the prince, taking control and shaping the world to his liking.

Today she'd taken back a piece of the narrative, though. She'd sent half of her paycheck to the palace. At least this way no one could say she'd taken more from Kostas than she was owed.

A knock sounded on her door, followed by a raised voice claiming to be from some blog site. She closed her eyes as she slid down the wall of her apartment. She would not answer…but they'd effectively trapped her.

Her finger itched to call Kostas…but pride stilled it. She was fine; she was fine. .

If you say it long enough, will it be true?

"What do you mean she sent part of her paycheck here?" Kostas pushed a hand through his hair. He'd started letting it grow back out after Calla's statements in The Grotto a few weeks ago. There'd been a few comments from people on the island and more than one cruel statement on social media calling it unprofessional. But he felt more like himself.

And Ioannis hadn't cared. He'd changed himself because of his own perception of expectations rather than what they actually were.

Natalia looked at the tablet in her hands and stated the sum before adding, "Based on my calculations, she'll have paid you back in full in the next six months."

"I don't need to be paid back."

Don't want it.

"Perhaps not, but if anyone asks, it will be good to show the record of her repaying it now that you two aren't together."

Natalia's crisp words struck Kostas. "What?"

She opened her mouth but Kostas stopped her. "No need to repeat, that was rhetorical."

Natalia nodded as she looked at her tablet again and started listing the day's events. He was scheduled at the clinic until four, which meant that Calla wouldn't be there.

He closed his eyes as that pain washed over him. In the three days since she'd walked out, she'd successfully avoided him in the one place they hadn't been able to escape each other for months. He'd pushed through his regular schedule, his body aching with hurt and need that he made sure not to show.

"There is a concert this weekend, benefiting..." Natalia frowned as she tapped a few things onto the tablet. "I just had it here."

Kostas waved a hand. "I'm not interested in attending a concert right now." He was stunned she'd even suggest it. He was barely managing to do the things he had to do. If he could've gotten away with calling off at the clinic for a week, he would. But duty and responsibility...

Duty and responsibility. The words tasted bitter, even though they remained unspoken.

"Oh." Natalia pursed her lips and dragged her finger up on the electronic planner. "Eleni mentioned you might not be interested in things for a while, but you seem so fine."

Fine? He looked at his assistant. She was serious. How could she be serious? Surely, he wasn't that good of an actor...his mask wasn't that secure. Was it?

"Where is Eleni this morning?"

"It's breakfast time, so probably with the children in their rooms. They like to do a relaxed—"

"Thanks, Natalia," Kostas called as he hustled to his brother and sister-in-law's suite. A hard bubble of truth was settling under his skin, and he wanted to confirm it with someone he could trust.

"Good morning, Kostas." Eleni's voice was warm as she looked up from nursing Zelia.

"Do people not realize I'm heartbroken?" The question was awkward, but he couldn't pull it back or ask it better.

His world had fallen apart when Calla walked out. She'd let the press see her tears. He'd run his hand over the images, hating the pain, but uncertain what he should do.

He'd kept up the regal face. The images captured showed a doctor in control, a man exiting the clinic on time. Going about his day, as always. But he was still devastated.

"No. You hide behind your mask well, Kostas. I wasn't sure until now."

If the mask could fool his sister-in-law, what about Calla?

She softened her tone as she looked at him. "You control so much that the world doesn't see you. They see Prince Kostas."

Control.

He'd tried to control everything since returning to the island. He'd promised himself that no one would find fault with him. And that if they made something up, he'd rebut it.

But it wasn't real. Who he was with Calla was the real Kostas. And he'd let that go for—what?—an image he didn't even want.

His father had failed to listen to his mother. To hear what she wanted. And he'd done the same. Unintentionally and with much better motives. But that didn't change the fact that he'd hurt the woman he loved.

"I need to see Calla." He turned without waiting for a response.

Just before he heard the door close, Kostas caught Eleni's whispered, "About time."

* * *

"Prince Kostas, what are you doing here?"

"Seeing the woman I love and begging forgiveness." He saw a few heads pop up at that statement and hated that it was surprise coating them. It was oddly freeing to say exactly what he wanted rather than couch it.

They shouted a few more questions at him as he hit the top of the stairs. He knocked on Calla's door and his heart broke as she called through, "No comment."

A few cameras followed, and he knew they were capturing this moment. But for the first time in his life, he didn't care. He loved Calla. He wanted everyone to know it, full stop.

"It's me, Calla."

He waited, the silence stretching as he leaned his head against her door, aware of the additional eyes watching him.

"No comment," Calla called again, but there was a hiccup of a sob behind it.

"Fine. I'll sit outside this apartment until we talk. We can even talk through the door, sweetheart. But I'm not giving up." He slid down the door.

He waved to the camera as he leaned back. He was a man in love, and he was determined that no one was going to doubt that. Most especially the woman on the other side of the door.

"That will make quite the story." Her voice

was soft, but he could still hear her. She must be sitting right by the door.

"Maybe." He responded. "But I don't care what the story is. I love you, and that is the only story that matters. And if the only people that ever know it are the two of us, then that is enough. I'm done caring what the headline or narrative is." He didn't shout the words, but he didn't whisper them, either.

Let the world know the truth. All he cared was that Calla heard him. That she knew he loved her.

The lock clicked and he couldn't stop the grin from spreading across his face. Standing, he opened the door, sliding inside. His breath caught as he saw her sitting on the floor next to the door, tears streaming down her face.

"Calla." He bent next to her.

"I'm fine, Kostas. Or I will be. Don't worry, I won't let them see me break. At least not like this, promise."

He brushed away a tear, his heart shattering at the sight of the woman he loved hurting. Worried about how it looked to someone else. He'd done this. His quest for perfection, even though he'd said he didn't care about the narrative anymore...part of her still wasn't sure.

"Calla, I am so sorry. I don't need perfection, honey. I just need you." He reached for her hands, grateful when she let him hold them. It was more than he deserved.

"I love you. I should have said that when we fought. Hell, I should have said it the moment I realized it. Should have told you then shouted it to the world. I don't have a good excuse for why I didn't. Fear. The need to protect myself. A lifetime of keeping things inside."

Calla's bright eyes lit up as she looked at him. "You love me, not who I could be or because I'm carrying your child?" She hiccupped as she looked at him.

"Just you." He placed a hand over where their child slept. "I love this little guy or gal too. But it's their mother that I'm here for. I want to be a team, Calla. A real one."

Calla threw her hands around Kostas's shoulders. "I love you too." She kissed him before pulling back.

Pursing her lips, she stood, looking at the door and then back at him. "But I also owe you an apology. That is a lot!" She gestured to the door. "I've done my best to handle it, but…"

"Your best was pretty great." He dropped a kiss to her nose.

"Maybe for a day or so. Over the long term…" Calla glared at the door. "I am not saying we have to refute everything, but I also understand your desire to.

"I let the trauma of my past cloud my present. I was so worried that you'd find fault with me eventually. That the narrative was meant for me, not them. That I wasn't enough. I'm sorry."

"Oh, Calla. You will always be enough." He brushed his lips against hers.

"I have something for you." Kostas grinned as he slid to one knee. "Calla Lewis, will you marry me?" He flipped open a ring box, watching carefully how Calla's eyes brightened.

"It's a different ring." She beamed as her eyes looked at the ring. "Oh, it's beautiful. Yes, Kostas. Yes, I will marry you."

He took the ring from the box and slid it on her finger. The diamond was smaller, and it had two sapphires on either side. It was gorgeous, reminding him so much of Calla the moment he'd seen it.

Maybe it wasn't large, and it wouldn't be easily identifiable in pictures like the other, but it was meant for her. And that was all that mattered.

Dropping his lips to hers, he relaxed as she slid into him. The world was simply right when she was in his arms.

EPILOGUE

THE PHONE IN the clinic rang for the hundredth time in the last hour, and Dr. Bandi sighed. They had to keep the phone on in case a patient needed them, but the calls were only the press. The front desk assistant had been instructed to give no updates on the royal baby.

"I swear they are calling more now than they did for Eleni's delivery," Calla muttered as Kostas wiped her brow.

"Well, they love you, sweetheart," Kostas whispered in her ear. "Love" was too strong of a word, but Kostas's declaration of love outside her door had changed the tone of most of the reporting. They might never be granted the grace that Ioannis and Eleni had, but no one doubted that Kostas and Calla loved each other.

Another contraction started and Calla squeezed Kostas's hand, aware she was probably being too forceful but...

"Push, Princess."

"Alexa, if you call me that one more time, I

will—" Calla groaned as she bore down. The contraction subsided as she laid her head back against Kostas, releasing her death grip on his fingers—which he flexed without complaining.

He'd climbed into bed with her when she'd started pushing. It was sweet and comforting, but she was so ready to be done. To hold her child and rest.

"Sorry, Pr—" Alexa caught herself as Calla shot her a glare.

Dr. Bandi looked up. "You're almost there. A few more pushes."

"A few more pushes." Calla moaned. "You keep saying that!" She took a deep breath as the next contraction started.

"You've got this, honey." Kostas kissed her cheek as she squeezed his hands and pushed. His fingers must be screaming, but he hadn't complained at all.

The pressure released and Calla sighed as the doctor looked up.

"They've got a full head of hair! One more push, Calla."

Bearing down, she followed the instructions and let out a sob as the doctor placed her squealing daughter against her chest.

"She's nearly perfect." Kostas whispered as he kissed the top of Calla's head.

"Nearly perfect?" Calla opened her mouth and made a face at her husband before kissing

the top of her daughter's head. "Nearly perfect" had become their running joke in the last few months. Calla might not like the term "perfect" but "nearly perfect" she'd accepted. And Kostas used it as often as possible.

"Would you prefer perfect? Seems like a lot to lay on a newborn still covered in vernix, but…"

"Nearly perfect, she is." Calla closed her eyes as she soaked in the first few minutes of their daughter's life. They were a family of three now.

Her nearly perfect little family.

* * * * *

If you enjoyed this story, check out these other great reads from Juliette Hyland

The Vet's Unexpected Houseguest
A Nurse to Claim His Heart
Reawakened at the South Pole
The Pediatrician's Twin Bombshell

All available now!